REV

THE REV WARRIORS SERIES

T.R. HARRIS

BOOK 1

Copyright 2018 by T.R. Harris

All rights reserved, without limiting the rights under copyright reserved above, no part of this publication may be reproduced, stored in or introduced into a retrieval system, or transmitted, in any form, or by any means (electronic, mechanically, photocopying, recording, or otherwise) without the prior written permission of both the copyright owner and the above publisher of this book. This is a work of fiction. Names, characters, places, brands, media and incidents are either the product of the author's imagination or are used fictitiously. ***

EMAIL

Please sign up to be included on the master email list to receive updates and announcements regarding the series, including release notices of upcoming books, purchase specials and more, please fill out the **Subscribe** form below:

Subscribe to Email List

CONTACT THE AUTHOR

Email: *bytrharris@hotmail.com*

Website: bytrharris.com

NOVELS BY T.R. HARRIS

The Human Chronicles Saga – Continuum
Mission Critical (An Adam Cain Adventure)

The Human Chronicles Saga (original series)
The Fringe Worlds
Alien Assassin
The War of Pawns
The Tactics of Revenge
The Legend of Earth
Cain's Crusaders
The Apex Predator
A Galaxy to Conquer
The Masters of War
Prelude to War
The Unreachable Stars
When Earth Reigned Supreme
A Clash of Aliens
Battlelines

The Copernicus Deception
Scorched Earth
Alien Games
The Cain Legacy
The Andromeda Mission
Last Species Standing
Invasion Force
Force of Gravity

REV Warriors Series
REV
REV: Renegades

Jason King – Agent to the Stars Series
The Enclaves of Sylox
Treasure of the Galactic Lights

The Drone Wars Series
Day of the Drone
In collaboration with George Wier…
The Liberation Series
Captains Malicious

Available exclusively on **Amazon.com**
and **FREE** to members of **Kindle Unlimited.**

REV

The Beginning

NOTES

Limited function biobots, controlled with attractant chemotaxis, are used to temporarily enhance and balance specific hormones in those individuals capable of surviving pre-NT-4 screening and training. Successful graduates of the Program have life expectancy—or length of active duty—based on their body's continuing ability to manage the stressors on specific organs.

- Dr. Clifford Slater (Basic NT-4 Considerations and Contraindications, Third Edition, 2083)

1

"You okay in there, gunny?"

Gunnery Sergeant Zac Murphy craned his neck so he could see his squad commander—Captain Tom Keller—through the tiny window in the pod. "Snug as a bug, sir," he replied with a smile. "Anxious to get some alien blood on my hands. It's been a while."

"Patience; another fifteen minutes and you'll be neck deep in the stuff."

"You promise? Don't be teasing me, sir. You know what happens when I get mad."

The last sentence was a standing joke within the unit, and one based more on reality than bravado.

"Just keep it pointed in the right direction, sergeant, and I'll be happy."

"Yes, sir."

Zac was ensconced inside an eight-meter-long, by three-meter-wide pod called an Ejection Capsule (EC), locked down, plugged in and five minutes from drop. Through the narrow viewport inches from his face, he glimpsed men from the RU—the recovery unit—loading into a landing shuttle in the next station over. They would follow him to the surface only minutes behind. After that, the main Marine force would sweep in through the breach—if there was a breach—and do the cleanup.

Nothing like having the weight of the entire operation riding on your shoulders....

Captain Keller was encased in his battle armor as well, ready to lead the RU to the surface. He leaned in closer to the window. "Thirty seconds to initial boost…three minutes to drop."

Zac nodded as best he could inside his battle helmet. The grey metal headrest was secured to the form-fitting body cushion lining the back of the capsule, so it was only his head that moved. His movements were also restricted by the thin, fused metal collar he wore around his neck which would administer the drugs as the mission proceeded. It also contained his battle computer. There were four tiny cameras embedded in the collar—two looking forward and two back. They would transmit real-time video of the Run, both for operational archives and debrief. He also had thin transducer wires plugged into the back of his skull, allowing subconscious instructions to be relayed should they become necessary. On a conscious level, he would be oblivious to the commands, but his instincts would obey—at least to a point. The computer would also track his ammo usage and signal the various stages of the assault.

Two other men appeared outside the capsule, crowding out the Marine officer, each waving one-finger salutes through the thick plate-glass viewport. Captain Keller grinned and gave them the right-of-way.

"Semper Fi, *mo-fo!*" they yelled in unison. "Don't let your wheelchair get in the way, old man. You're a pitiful excuse for a

Marine! Your momma should have drowned you at birth. I thought she did!"

"You sick bastards!" Zac shot back. "Just wait until I get back. They'll be some major ass whooping when I do."

Corporal Danny Gains and Staff Sergeant Manny Hernandez waved their hands in mock horror. "Watch out, *Jog*," Hernandez said. "He might come back and beat us over the head with his cane."

This was a ritual all REVs followed; a promise to return from the near-suicidal Run to the safety of the ship, if only to seek revenge for the insults. It was all good-natured taunting in the face of incredible danger.

There were only three REVs aboard the huge battle-carrier *Olympus*, making for a small, tight-knit group with their own rituals and nomenclature. Danny was the *Jogger*—Jog—a rookie with less than ten Runs to his name. Manny had a couple of dozen under his belt and was called *Bolt*. Zac was the most-senior of the small cadre. He was a *Ram*, having earned his horns long before the other two even joined the Corps. In fact, he was…

Zac felt a slight pinch on the back of his neck as the first of the pre-drugs was administered, a variant of dopamine and other proprietary ingredients. A feeling of calm swept over him. He looked out at his companions with a silly grin on his face.

"He's gone," Manny said, as the humor vanished from his voice and expression.

Captain Keller returned to the view plate.

"Confirm status," he ordered solemnly.

"Status green," Zac mumbled. "Standing by."

Keller nodded. This initial injection was just the warmup,

something to make the ride to the surface more bearable. Once on the planet, he'd get the good stuff—and that's when the real show would begin.

A panel in the bulkhead spiraled open and the EC slid inside. It was pitch black in the chamber, with the only light coming from the dim Heads-Up Display that flashed on once the capsule was placed in the launch tube. Zac was alone now. He wasn't afraid or apprehensive; he preferred it this way. It was safer for everyone involved.

"Drop in ten," said Keller's voice through the comm speakers in Zac's helmet. "Good luck, gunny. See you on the other side."

"Roger that, sir." Zac was feeling giddy now, as if he didn't have a care in the world. "Yippee-ki-yay, mother—"

The air was suddenly sucked out of his lungs as the tiny pod shot from the side of the battle-carrier. It received a major acceleration boost from the mag-rails, before falling of its own accord through the thin upper atmosphere of ES-8. Tiny air jets controlled the angle of entry, and moments later, the view through the pressure window was streaked with brilliant torrents of yellow and red flame.

The drugs in Zac's system helped him endure the nine-g entry and violent buffeting taking place without passing out…or losing his lunch. Even then, this was his one hundred fourth drop, and if it wasn't for the brief duration of the transit, he would have fallen asleep on the ride down.

Four minutes later, the assault capsule entered the lower atmosphere and began to slow down. Stubby wings extended from the fuselage, providing more control for the transition toward the landing zone.

It would be early morning at the LZ—two hours before sunrise; even so it was a good bet the Qwin were already tracking his approach. Any minute now they would send a variety of flak in his direction. The threat-avoidance system of the EC was one of the most-advanced, and in all the history of orbital drops of this sort, only twenty-four had been taken out by enemy countermeasures prior to landing. Out of over two thousand sorties, that wasn't a bad percentage. Unfortunately, Zac had known seven of the REVs who bought it, so he was aware that at any time his check could get cashed. Hell, even aliens got lucky now and then.

The pod suddenly shifted course to avoid a series of roiling balls of plasma lifting up from the surface. Zac gnashed his teeth and took in a few quick breaths to compensate for the extreme g-forces that slammed his body from side to side in his restrictive container. Then within a second, the pod dropped straight down several thousand feet, pulling Zac's stomach into his throat. The landing drugs were good, but even they had limits. Blood trickled from Zac's nose and splattered on the faceplate of his helmet. Sensors detected the obstruction and a chemical agent on the glass burned away the red liquid.

Zac watched with almost hypnotic intensity as the concentric squares on the HUD cycled relentlessly toward the LZ. The pod jogged again, following a jagged course toward the ground, dancing between ballistic balls of fire sent from the surface.

Two more contacts appeared, causing alarms to sound within the capsule. These were tracking missiles and much harder to avoid. Zac often wondered why alarms were needed to warn him of the weapons. He was at the mercy of the pod's guidance computer and helpless to do anything to affect its course. Perhaps the alarms were there to let him know he was in some really *deep* shit now, rather than just your ordinary run-of-the-mill *shallow* shit....

The evasive maneuvers became even more abrupt and erratic, as the computer directed diversionary countermeasures to explode from the surface of the pod. Most were tiny drones, designed to mimic the signature of the entry capsule. Others carried heat sources which would ionize the near-by atmosphere and confuse the pressure readers on the ground and in the missiles. The missiles changed course, leaving the EC falling even faster toward the surface.

Once Zac dropped below five thousand feet, the capsule would be safe from this particular type of defensive system. After that, everything sent by the Qwin would be aimed at him personally.

As the capsule dropped lower, Zac knew the time was near. He readied himself for the change....

Unlike the entry drugs, Zac didn't feel the NT-4 when it was injected into his system—that was the idea, no feelings at all—but for a moment he was aware of its presence. A jolt of electric energy and savage strength surged through every part of his body as his biology cascaded, so all-consuming and frenetic that it evoked the primal scream endemic to REVs everywhere. Through the comm, the Marines on the orbiting battle-carrier heard the blood-curdling shriek. At that moment Gunnery Sergeant Zac Murphy was no longer the man they'd known only a few minutes before.

He was now a REV.

The landing came with an abrupt deceleration as the pod shifted orientation to a steep forty-five degree angle. Just as the bottom skids contacted the surface, two sharp titanium blades extended below the capsule, designed to plow into the soil and slow the vehicle. A huge cloud of dust and dirt marked the passage of the EC as it chewed through small hills and fields of grass and dark soil. The parallel tracks left by the blades pointed directly at a large dam and hydroelectric-conversion complex holding back a massive lake. It had once provided power to the alien city fifteen klicks away, which spanned a wide valley between two modest rows of grassy hills. If Zac had awareness, he would have found the scene pleasing, even tranquil. As it was, he felt no such emotion. All he felt was rage.

Even before the cloud of dust could catch up to the pod, the forward section blew off, sending Zac soaring into the air. With the momentum of the landing and the force of his ejection, he reached the grassy surface next to a drainage river already in full stride, sprinting across the star-lit ground in a blur. His right arm was encased in an M-93 auto pulse-rifle and on his left, a Mod-9 grenade/flamethrower unit. When added to his body armor and natural weight, Zac carried a load of just under five hundred pounds.

The field around him exploded in geysers of gunfire as the Qwin released round after round in his direction from defensive batteries placed along the higher levels of the dam. The matte gray of his armor and the electronic jammers in his collar made him a hard target to track, allowing him to deftly dodge the incoming fire. He covered the remaining one hundred-eighty meters of open terrain in nine seconds flat.

A week before, the aliens had abandoned the nearby city, left in ruins and darkened by the Qwin's savage revenge against their once-loyal Enif followers who now sided with the Humans. They occupied the settlement initially, until ships from Earth arrived and began flooding the streets with killer drones and raining bombardments down on them from space. The vast size of the power plant, along with miles of internal passageways within the dam, offered protection and a base of operations as the aliens and their remaining native allies regrouped. It was Zac's job to make sure they didn't get too comfortable in their new surroundings.

As he approached the barricaded entrance to the sprawling complex, he sighted a squad of Qwin and Enif flanking the main gate. Q-90's mounted on tripods whirled in his direction. Zac lifted the Mod-9 and launched four grenades at the alien positions while continuing his headlong race to the gate. That was the purpose of a Run—not to stop. His job was to penetrate enemy lines and create chaos within the ranks, prompting a panicked retreat. The main Marine force would then pour in and herd the enemy farther into their hideout. There they would be trapped or attempt to escape into space. Waiting buzzships would do the clean up after that.

But it was Zac's job to get the ball rolling.

He was at the gate by the time the grenades exploded, taking out the defensive units. The exterior security force was insignificant compared to what was about to hit them in the form of an activated REV. Not every assault was led by a REV, but now that Zac was on the surface, the news would spread quickly and strategies would change.

Zac lowered a shoulder and barreled through the gate like it wasn't there.

Within the open grounds outside the main generator building, other aliens had quickly assembled an interior defense line behind concrete barricades. There were about a hundred of them, all Qwin, and experienced fighters from the look of their organized formation. Zac's HUD detected the heat signatures of the aliens as his mind locked in their locations. The performance-enhancing drug coursing through his system improved memory, even as his body and mind operated on autopilot. As it was with most advanced Savants, they didn't have to think about solutions to complex equations—the answers simply appear to them. Under the influence of NT-4, it was the same with Zac. He was operating on pure instinct; conscious thought would have only slowed him down. Now his blistering eye/hand coordination did all the work. Without realizing it, his M-93 was spitting white-hot lead at the Qwin. His reaction time was faster than anything other than full computer-assist, but that required a stationary platform and a full array of detectors to operate efficiently. Zac didn't need any outside help. And he was also mobile, almost too mobile for the aliens to follow. He swept the area with his weapon, sending shattered and bloodied body parts exploding into the air. In six seconds, the area was clear of enemy combatants.

He detected two wounds to his body, one along the outer thigh of his right leg, and another on his left shoulder. Most of his armor was still intact, and neither injury impeded his attack in the slightest, so he ignored them offhand.

The remaining Qwin retreated into the main building leading to the dam, running under huge pipes and conduits, and around towering circular generators. Zac didn't hesitate and followed them inside.

Although still locked together and operational, his armor was becoming pitted with dents from the alien ballistics, and occasionally his electronics would flicker from a strike of plasma energy. The suit was designed to withstand such punishment and to counter any electrical overloads, but like all things, it had its limits. Within the interior of the complex, those limits would be tested.

Zac was much faster than the fleeing aliens, even with his heavy pack, and soon he was blasting the creatures at point-blank range as he ran by. This particular squad—the remaining force from outside, was soon neutralized, leaving the units farther in the complex to form up defensive lines in the cavernous energy distribution area within the dam.

This was where the main conduits joined, allowing the natives to control the production and distribution of power to the city. There were ample hiding places for the Qwin, and they seemed to have every one of them utilized.

Zac unleashed a combined stream of thick, yellow flame from one arm, and the relentless scream of lead from his M-93 on the other, covering a full one hundred-eighty degrees of the room in front of him. He took more fire himself, but shrugged it off. There would be time enough to heal after the Run, if he survived it.

The aliens broke off and ran deeper into the complex. Zac followed, easily overtaking the runners while barreling through hastily constructed barricades and defenses. The Qwin could barely turn over a table to hide behind before Zac was upon them. Seeing this, most of the aliens no longer bothered. They just ran.

"What the hell is he doing?" Lieutenant Colonel Paul Owens cried out. He ran up beside Captain Tom Keller. Both officers had running data streams on their HUDs, chronicling the progress of the Run.

Keller knew what Owens was referring to. *Two klicks.*

"I know," he huffed as he ran. "Time at seven minutes, forty-five."

"At that pace he'll outrun his RU—and his backup."

"Maybe less resistance?"

"Not according to mission stats. Rate of fire and tentative body count puts this at one the highest."

Tom placed a small quadrant screen on his HUD and linked it to one of Zac's collar video monitors. The REV was still blasting forward, killing aliens and moving forward through wide hallways and into cavernous workrooms. The aliens were everywhere, although most of the ones Keller could see on the screen were dead.

He checked the distance to target. Point four of a klick and increasing. Zac was running away from his support team and deeper into enemy territory.

At the ten minute mark, Zac was two-point-nine klicks into the complex, having run the full width of the dam and into tunnels placed within the solid rock of the opposite mountain wall—and a full klick ahead of the RU. He could be Twilighted anytime between now and twelve minutes into the Run, depending on his vitals. Keller scanned them on his HUD. The bastard was all in the green. This one was going the distance.

Suddenly Zac stopped. The view on Keller's HUD showed Zac stand upright and rigid, before toppling to the ground. The camera view was static, pointing ahead at ground level at a large, dark passageway forty feet away.

Keller checked Zac's readouts. It wasn't the Twilight, and neither was he dead. All indicators were still in the green.

Through the remote camera, the Marine captain saw dozens of Qwin rush from the shadows, all converging on Zac. The aliens knew what was happening—or at least they thought they did. Here was a Twilighted REV with his backup woefully behind. They would rip Zac to shreds.

Just then, flares of gunfire erupted from Zac's M-93. The line of fire raked across the advancing line, literally cutting the aliens in half at the waistline. Dozens died in an instant, while sending the few survivors racing for cover.

The camera angle shifted as Zac got to his feet and began to follow.

The two Marine officers exchanged baffled looks, before rejoining their running troops.

Zac noticed something odd about his left arm; it wasn't working anymore. He felt no pain, just the drag on his body from the now useless flame-thrower and grenade launcher dangling at his side. His battle computer triggered a release lever on the left arm of his suit. The armor fell away, along with the armament, lightening his load and allowing him to gain an ounce more speed.

He sprinted through another long tunnel and into a large chamber before racing across toward an opening where the aliens were running. Then he heard the three chimes.

Even in his frenzied state, instinct continued to guide his actions. He didn't think what the chines meant, he just reacted to them. They were the five-second warning before Twilight.

With a Pavlov-like reaction to the sound, Zac set about clearing the area of all living things, expending round after round in a deadly circle of fire around where he stood. He still had a few rounds left when his body suddenly went rigid again and fell to the ground.

Second-Insir Basno Vin watched the Human creature fall to the floor of the chamber. He turned to his cadre and warned them back. The crazed killing machine had done this earlier; this could be yet another deception.

He peered to the other side of the chamber, watching and

listening for signs of other Humans. In normal circumstances, they would be there, rushing forth to secure their fallen weapon. Yet there was only silence, punctuated by the baying of Basno's wounded and dying all around.

This killer had acted differently, resulting in another sub-cadre being slaughtered. Basno was taking no chances.

He signaled for four of his troops to flank the creature to the right. He would crawl through the cover of the many bodies on the floor and approach from the left, hoping his faith in the Order would protect him.

The going was sickening, as he moved through the pools of blood and sinew that had once been his cadre companions. With each *olen* he moved, the desire grew within him to sever a piece of the Human beast for his collection, especially this one. This beast had killed more Antaere than any he'd seen before. But now he lay inert on the concrete, an inviting target, if possibly a deceptive one.

A loud blast of gunfire startled Basno from his reverie. He glanced to his right to see his four-cad squad cut to pieces. He glared back at the creature the Humans called a REV, snarling as he did. Yet the body still lay unconscious on the floor.

More gunfire…and this time Basno identified the source, as Human fighters entered the chamber from the far side. Glancing back, he saw his other cadre scurrying away, deeper in the complex. He was alone.

Grabbing a half-torso and blown off arm of one of his companions, Basno covered himself with the carcass. He would not get out of the chamber alive—that was evident. As such, his last duty to the Order was to exterminate the highest ranking enemy officer he could locate. He pulled his weapon in close to his body, looking ahead of him at the unconscious REV warrior. Senior officers would come to him; they always did. And that would be when Basno committed his final act of devotion to his race.

Members of the Recovery Unit ran up to Zac and surrounded him, as hundreds of armored Marines poured into the chamber and rushed off after the fleeing Qwin. Captain Tom Keller was one of the first to arrive at Zac's side. Still panting from the long and fast run, he dropped to his knees and cradled Zac's bloody head in his hands. Half the helmet was shattered, and there was a long, angry gash along Zac's right cheek. His left arm was a bruised and bloody sock of shattered bones and from the double holes in his left leg, Tom wondered how he could stand, let alone carry out a Run of devastating effectiveness.

The med crew laid out a stabilizing gurney. It was designed to roll over bodies and other obstacles while providing a level ride for the patient. It also had a variety of drugs and plasma containers built into the rails. This was the critical period, when the level of NT-4 had to be brought down as quickly as possible before the REV burned out. But it was also NT-4 that allowed the body to function as such high levels. The Twilight drug helped, as did the other drug cocktail soon to be administered. The Catch-22 was obvious: how much drug to keep in the system to help him survive. But the med-techs knew their job. They asked a couple of the other Marines to help them lift him onto the gurney.

"Damn, is he still alive?" one of the Marines asked.

A med-tech had already slapped a couple of Wi-Fi monitors to his chest and temple and was tracking his vitals. "Still ticking," he said. "Pulse strong, EEG active. He's Twilighted but his mind is working. Probably still on the Run in his mind, killing more aliens."

"*Oorah!*" the Marine called out, which was picked up by several others within ear shot.

"Knock it off," Keller ordered. "Get him out of here and to the staging area. He's got a lot of healing to do. Let's get him started ASAP."

Keller stood up and watched his twelve-person EU crew move Zac's unconscious body from the chamber. He glanced around the room. The floor was covered with the bodies of alien dead. It had been like this all along the course of the Run. *This is one for the record books*, he thought.

Then his eyes locked on those of another.

The alien was staring at him, with no signs of pain or anguish on his pale yellow face. Instead, his eyes were cold and sober, with even a slight grin on his face

Pop! Pop!

Keller jumped at the sound. For a moment he sensed his body, trying to tell if he'd been shot. That wasn't always evident right away, and from the wicked look on the alien's face, he wouldn't be surprised to find a bloody hole in his body somewhere, disguised by shock.

"I got him, captain!" yelled a young Marine. He was part of the main brigade under Owens' command, so Tom didn't know his name. "Fucker had a bead on you, too, sir." The barrel of the M-101 was still aimed at the dead alien in the floor.

"Thank you, Marine. You did well." Keller's knees were like rubber. *That was close.* "Grab a couple of your buddies and check the others. No more surprises, okay?"

"Yes sir!"

The Marines—along with a generous helping of Army Rangers—were in the process of landing in a steady stream of shuttlecraft, filling up most of the wide plane outside the complex. Mobile Assault Vehicles (MAVs), with mounted 80s, were forming up and preparing to enter the complex. Captain Tom Keller was always impressed with the speed and efficiency of the securing procedure, how so much equipment and personnel could be dropped on a surface of an alien world and immediately set to work. It made him proud to be a Marine.

But his distraction was fleeting. A large medical shuttle was already on the surface with Zac inside. Before experiencing the various stresses associated with transition to orbit, Zac had to be checked out thoroughly and stabilized. It wouldn't do to have a fractured rib slice through the chest cavity during a period of turbulence or rapid acceleration. The shuttle had all the facilities aboard to keep Zac alive, if it was possible.

Colonel Owens intercepted him as he was entering the shuttle.

"How's your patient, Tom?" he asked.

Keller had his battle helmet tucked under his left arm, so he had no access to the HUD and its link to Zac's vitals. "He's alive, that's about all I know. What's the initial mission sitrep?"

Owens let out a loud breath. "Your boy racked up another six hundred-plus kills. The remaining Qwin and a few of their devoted followers tried to get out along the mountain ridge to the south. Looks like about fifty prisoners, the rest are KIA."

"*Oorah*," Keller said half-heartedly. He loved the idea of a shitload of dead aliens, but at the moment he was more concerned with Zac.

"*Oorah*," Owens repeated. He looked hard at Keller. "You know we'll have to get to the bottom of this."

Keller nodded.

Colonel Owens pulled out a datapad and turned it on. "REVs *never* stop during a Run unless their mobility is affected. Murphy was on the ground for seventeen seconds without moving. How is that even possible while activated?"

"I don't know. But you're right…we need answers, and the only person who has them is in the shuttle fighting for his life. I'll ask him…if he survives."

NOTES

NT-3a Procedures and Conventions (First Edition)
Dr. Clifford Slater (Earlier report dated 2067)

Subject: Failures experienced most often during Program Training and Subject Evaluation: Subsequent Protocols.

Training personnel and medical supervisors should pay particular attention to the early signs of the following conditions (attached). Any candidate for the Program, or active operator, must be immediately pulled from training, or from active duty, at any occurrence of these failures or symptoms. Immediate cessation of training, or active operations, is required. Under no circumstances is additional NT-3a or pre-drugs to be administered to these individuals.

The following conditions are noted:

    1. *Avulsion fracture....*

2

As always when waking from a Twilight coma, Zac became fully aware the moment the counter drugs were introduced. He relaxed when he took a look around. He was on a hospital bed, surrounded by all the familiar accoutrements, either plugged into him or filling the room. There was even the lab-coated physician and a couple of cute and attentive nurses—along with one full-bird colonel.

"Welcome back, Marine," said the square-jawed man with the short, white hair.

Zac recognized him as Col. Jack Diamond, head of the 91st Regiment, the intelligence division. Zac knew the officer; he was fellow REV Manny Hernandez's uncle on his mother's side. Even so, why was a spook at his awakening?

"Thank you, sir," Zac whispered with a grimace. Although his senses were sharp and alert, his throat was as dry as the Sahara. One of the nurses helped him down a cupful of thick liquid. It helped.

"Great job back on Enif; chalk another one up for the good guys," Diamond said.

"*Oorah*, sir. So we won?"

Although in a crazed killing haze while under the influence of NT-4, a welcome side-effect was that afterwards a REV could recall every moment as if it happened in slow motion. If required, Zac could provide an accurate body count of every alien he killed. He already knew the outcome of the mission, and the colonel knew he did.

However, the one aspect of the mission—and the most troublesome for all REVs—was what happened *after* the Twilight drug was administered.

It was discovered years before that it was too dangerous for REVs to work within close proximity of their fellow Marines. While under the influence, anything that moved was a potential target, even friendlies. That's why people like Zac were sent in first —and alone. They were the bunker-busters in this war, enhanced killing machines perfectly suited for ferreting out the aliens in their hideouts. But once the job was done, they needed to be subdued before the backup troops could enter. And it was during this Twilight Period—between the time the REV was put down and the support troops arrived—that they were the most vulnerable.

Zac would enter the Twilight knowing he'd fulfilled his mission. What he didn't know was if he'd ever wake up again.

Seeing that he was now resting comfortably in a hospital bed and being tended to by pretty nurses, Zac didn't have to worry about the Twilight period any longer, at least until the next mission.

But now his rehab would begin. Twilight—and the other associated diluting drugs—were designed to quickly lower the level of NT-4 in his system, then once the deadly effects were purged from his body, he would be allowed to awake from his drug-induced coma. No REV escaped a Run uninjured, and the doctors preferred conscious patients to comatose vegetables as the healing began.

With his near-perfect recall of the Run, he was aware he'd suffered some major damage. He sighed. Even with the enhanced healing provided by the small residual NT-4 left in his system, he knew it was going to take a while to get over his last Run.

He looked at his shattered left arm...and frowned. Missing was the requisite cast, replaced now by only a gauze bandage.

He looked at the lab-coated doctor. "I thought I broke my arm?"

Arnie Patel was the lead REV doctor aboard the carrier. He only had three patients under his care, and they kept him busy. If he wasn't prepping one for a Run, he was patching up another and monitoring the third for any signs of PTSD. Patel was good at what he did and Zac was grateful for it. He'd patched up Zac on five other occasions over the past eight months aboard the carrier. They were trusted friends by now.

"You did," said the doctor.

There was something in Arnie's truncated answer that didn't sit right with Zac.

"Unless you guys have developed some kind of miracle broken arm ointment, where's the cast?"

"The fractures have healed, but not from any secret medical breakthrough."

"In seventy-two hours? You're shitting me?"

The normal time for a REV to be kept under after a mission was forty-eight to seventy-two hours, just enough time to reduce the NT-4 levels in the body. Zac tested his arm. It barely hurt; on second thought, it didn't hurt at all, except for the psychosomatic belief that it *should* hurt. Then it dawned on him. There was only one thing that could have done this....

"How long was I under?" He scanned the faces of the other people in the room. Most averted his eyes.

Arnie looked at Colonel Diamond. The officer nodded.

"Zac, we've had you under for ninety-four days," the doctor reported.

Zac's eyes grew wide, his mouth slack. "Ninety-four! Wha...why?" he stammered. "Was I that torn up?"

Arnie nodded. "Yeah, it was pretty bad."

The longest Zac had ever been kept in a drug-induced coma was fourteen days. The record for any REV—as far as he knew—was thirty-one, and that guy ended up dying from his wounds. But ninety-four days...and then there were the other considerations.

As a senior REV, Zac's body operated at a much higher metabolic level than normal people. His blood pressure was over two hundred, his body temperature and his heart rate all accelerated. It was NT-4—the Rev drug—that kept him alive, even at residual levels. And if he didn't get periodic dosages of combat level NT-4 to maintain his latent concentration, he would simply burn out. As a result, it became an unspoken reality that once a person passed the exhaustive—and dangerous—screening process and entered the Marines as an oh-351-E, he would be hooked on Rev for the rest of his life. Residual traces would always be present, which allowed them to survive where other people with their vitals would stroke out or suffer massive cardiac arrest.

Zac had gone over ninety days without a combat dose—and he was still alive. That wasn't right.

"It was the NT-4," Patel continued. "We had trouble purging it from your system."

"Why?"

"That's what we need to find out."

Col. Diamond stepped up to the bed. "The top scientist at the EDC is due here in five days," he said. The Enhancement Development Center was where NT-4 had first been designed for the military. "General McCabe will be arriving, too," the officer added.

"General Simon McCabe?" Zac stammered. "The theater commander?"

"That's the only General McCabe I know of, gunny."

"He's coming to see me?"

"In five days, so rest up," the colonel confirmed. He turned his attention to the room. "And get this man some real food in his stomach. This liquid mush you've been feeding him may be what his body *needs*, but it's not what a Marine *wants*." He looked at the doctor. "Get this man some meat…and that's an order."

Colonel Diamond was smiling when he left the room. He was the only who was.

Chicago Manual of Style, 34th Edition (2085): REV shall be capitalized in total when referring to individuals. The capitalized R-only Rev is the accepted slang for the enhancement drug NT-4.

3

An hour later, Zac was escorted on wobbly legs to the mess decks by four serious-looking and heavily-armed guards. It was customary for a couple to be his shadows for a few days after being revived, but not four…and after ninety-four days. By then, nearly every trace of Rev should've been flushed from his system. Even the residual amount a veteran REV of his longevity would be diminished after so long—which wasn't a good idea….

Even on short notice, word of Zac's awakening had spread throughout the ship, and when he arrived in the huge open-bay room—littered with dozens of bolted-down dining tables—the welcoming committee was waiting. After so long, much of the enthusiasm for his achievements during the Run had waned, but there was still a decent reception when he entered.

"*Oorah! Oorah! Oorah,*" the assembled Marines cheered. "Way to go Marine!"

As was also customary, Zac grinned widely and pumped his left fist up and down, acknowledging the respect and thanks from his fellow Marines. Without his incredible self-sacrifice, a fair number of them wouldn't be here today to cheer him, and they knew it.

Normally, he would have made the *peacock parade*—as it was called—only a week or two after the mission was completed, with the memory of the battle still fresh in everyone's minds. But ninety-four days was a long time in the life of a combat Marine. He wouldn't have been surprised to learn they'd taken part in another half-dozen assaults while he was under. The war with the Antaere and their fanatical followers was escalating, putting a strain on the troops currently on station within the Grid. New boots were coming, they just hadn't arrived yet. And even though there were two other REVs aboard the *Olympus* to pick up the load, Zac couldn't help feeling that on some level he'd let down his fellow Marines.

After the obligatory celebration died down, Zac took a seat at a table sequestered from the others, at a far end of the room. The guards took up positions, their eyes locked on his every movement.

REVs were subject to periodic flashbacks—a form of PTSD—which normally manifested within a couple of days after being revived, as trace amounts of the drug lingered in their bodies, adding to the residual. But after three months, he should be clear of any major effects. Not counting the danger to his system by not activating within that time, this was the longest he'd ever gone without making a Run, let alone receiving a maintenance boost. And four guards? What was that all about?

Captain Tom Keller approached the table; the guards let him pass. He slipped onto the bench on the other side of the table from Zac.

"Welcome back, Murphy," he greeted without smiling; in

fact, his tone was one of obvious concern. "We were wondering if you'd make it."

"Yeah, what the hell, captain?" said Zac. "Why was I under so long?"

"It's like Patel said, trying to purge the Rev from your system."

Zac leaned back. He stared at his unit commander for a moment before responding. "There's never been a problem before. Was there a screw up with the administration?"

Keller shook his head. "Everything's been checked out. We've had plenty of time to work through the possibilities, but still no definitive answers."

The two Marines were silent for a moment, each lost in the same thought: *Was this the end of Zac Murphy and his value to the Corps?*

"Listen, Cap, I'm not a burnout—"

"No one said you were, but after fifteen years, something was bound to give. Maybe you've built up a tolerance to the purging drugs. Or your tissue is hording NT longer and deeper. Those are some of the things Patel's talking about. We'll know more in a few of days when the doctor from the EDC gets here."

"Who's is it?" Zac asked. "David Cross is the head honcho there, has been for years."

"That's the one."

Zac raised his eyebrows. "No shit? He's been with the program since Slater's time—he was his intern. I've met him a couple of times, all REVs have. And he's coming all the way out here to see me?"

"Yep. Your stats have been constantly fed to Earth since the Run. They've been studying you for months. Now Colonel Cross is on his way."

"Could've just made a conference call, so why the personal visit?"

Tom shook his head. "Maybe he just missed your handsome mug."

"Yeah, I'm sure that's not it…sir."

Gunnery Sergeant Zachariah Murphy was the most-senior REV in the Corps, having been a part of the Program for over fifteen years. He was only the second person to go over twelve years, and then when the first REV to do so died—burned out actually—Zac became the longest living REV still on active duty. Since then, every day only added to the record.

Zac carried the Military Occupational Specialty code (MOS) of 0351-E, for Infantry Assault Marine-Enhanced. Within the MOS, there were three sub-designations: Alpha, Bravo and Charlie. The Alphas were the newbies, the boots, the test-tube babies, as the senior REVs called them. They were the zero- to four-year veterans of the Program. Three-fifty-one Bravos were the mid-tier REVs, at four to eight years. Zac was a Charlie, with eight-plus years as a REV. It was probably a good indicator about how the brass considered a REV with longevity, since Zac had already maxed out his special-designation pay—which sucked—and there was no scuttlebutt about adding a new letter for the more-senior REVs. There were only nine 'Charlies' in the Corps, and they weren't expected to last much longer.

That's what they said about Zac…seven years ago. Now it looked like they may have been right.

Every boy wanted to grow up to be a REV. They were the personification of the quintessential comic book superhero, incredibly strong, fast and tough, putting themselves out in front of the column to lead the Marines to victory over the evil aliens. As pillars of integrity, they were doing their part to vanquish the Qwin on a dozen distant worlds within the Grid. Rugged and handsome, they were also the epitome of masculinity.

Who *wouldn't* want to be a REV?

At least that's how the propaganda went.

Reality was a whole other thing.

REV warriors weren't recruited or trained. They were *discovered*. Since only a tiny fraction of the population could tolerate the stresses placed on the body by the drug, all were male, and only a sliver of those who volunteered for the Program made it through the screening process to become REVs. For some, NT-4 had very little effect, while an unfortunate few died at the first injection. Most simply went crazy and never came back down.

In the early days of the Program, this process was a hit or miss proposition. The fatality rate was unacceptably high which caused a major PR problem for the Corps. But as the years passed, procedures improved and warning signs identified. Now days, around twenty out of every thousand volunteers were advanced to the next stage, to the point where they actually experienced the awe and wonder that was NT-4.

In the second stage of screening, REV candidates were allowed a miniscule trace of NT-4 and under controlled conditions. At this point, the effects weren't noticeable for up to two days, after which eighty percent of the candidates wigged out or died. Those who didn't were moved to the next stage and given more. This was both a testing and conditioning phase. Although it had never been shown that people could develop a tolerance to NT-4, the body did learn to adapt to the symptoms, including the exceedingly high blood pressure, heart rate and body temperature. NT-4 helps the body to survive, even as it provides the impetus for such accelerated activity. After that, every person who enters the Fleet as a REV would die without periodic infusions of the drug.

A pair of stewards brought four plates of perfectly-marbled, sizzling steaks—and only steaks—to the table. The aroma would normally be intoxicating to a REV coming off Twilight, but Zac was too upset to notice.

"How's Olivia?" he asked Captain Keller, wanting to get his mind on something more pleasant.

Although personal relationships were frowned upon for REVs it was something that couldn't be avoided. REVs were perfect examples of the Human male. The drug allowed only necessary body fat, while defining muscle and creating rippling six-pack abs. Even those who didn't start off with square jaws and lean faces developed them over time. And then there was the danger factor, which was an intoxicant for some women. These were super men, with super bodies, who killed aliens for a living. The attraction was inevitable.

Hospital Corpsman 1st Class Olivia Contreras was Zac's on-again, off-again relationship. The variable nature depended on whether Zac was jacked-up on REV or recovering from a variety of injuries after a Run. This left them a very narrow window to get together. Olivia knew this better than most; she was Dr. Arnie Patel's chief assistant. Both she and Zac accepted reality for what it was. It kept them from getting too deep with their feelings.

Keller looked away. "She's been checking on you every day. She knows the seriousness of a ninety-day layoff for a REV—any

REV. The fact that they had trouble getting the levels down is probably why you're still alive."

"And she didn't find that an acceptable compromise?"

"Not in the least. You should go see her after you eat."

Zac looked at the watchful guards. "If they'll let me. Remember, I'm a menace-to-society."

"I'll see what I can do."

"How about ops while I was under?" Zac asked. "How'd my kids do?"

"Not bad. Hernandez got pretty beat up at another site on ES-8. Jog's been doing fine. He has potential to be one of the great ones." Keller smiled. "Like you."

"Flattery will get you…well, absolutely nothing at this point…sir." Zac's return smile was weak and insincere.

Keller continued. "We just came off Borin-Noc—ES-6—you know the place."

ES stood for Earth-Standard, and was one of the reasons humanity and the Antaere were at war. Each coveted Earth-like worlds, which had brought the aliens to Earth in the first place. Out of the three hundred-plus habitable worlds discovered within the thousand light-year sphere of space known as the Grid, only twelve were perfect matches for humanity's home-world, in terms of gravity, atmosphere, radiation levels and more. The Qwin—a derogatory term for the Antaere use by just about everybody—had made inroads on all ES worlds over the past hundred years, spreading their religion called The Order and indoctrinating trillions of beings. Yet as the aliens interacted more with the natives, their promise of Universal Order began to look more like universal slavery. But none dared rise up against the aliens and their superior technology, not until the Humans came on the scene and offered an ally with the skills to defy the Qwin.

Beginning with kicking the Qwin off Earth, Humans now had military operations running on four of the twelve ES worlds. The going was tough, since even the natives who wished to be free of the aliens were afraid to fully commit to the effort. It was more than liberating territory; minds also had to be freed. The mystical nature of the Order caused many to pause and not join in the fight. Instead, they were content to let the Humans do the fighting for them. Not surprising, this suited the military just fine. Most natives were atrocious fighters, lacking the skill, instincts and technology to make a serious contribution.

Yet the Antaere still controlled the bulk of the ES worlds, with their religious tentacles thread throughout every layer of multiple civilizations. The Humans were making progress, but it was a slow and bloody slog, and with the constant threat of a Qwin counterattack on Earth. The Antaere spoke of this often, which kept the Human military in a constant state of preparedness. Only by creating a wide enough buffer around the Earth would humanity feel safe.

"Are the Qwin back on Borin?"

"They tried," Keller replied. "We had to call in the 45th to help out. The aliens are still there, but confined to a small part of the southern hemisphere. We'll bring in nukes if the engineers can't get them out."

"That would be a waste of prime real estate, sir. Won't that also violate the Assistance Clause with the natives?"

"The Borin seem okay with it. It seems people are beginning to see what sick bastards the Qwin are. Humans are in vogue these days, as far as Knights in Shining Armor go. Besides, we can't leave the yellow rat-bastards with a foothold this close to Earth."

Keller looked at the four thick steaks. His stomach growled.

"You better get to work on those…before I take them off your hands."

Zac smiled. "I'd like to see you cash four huge steaks in one sitting…sir."

"So would I, gunny, so would I."

He left Zac to his meal.

Zac wolfed through the first four steaks and ordered another. With his high metabolism, he needed a lot of calories to maintain his body weight. During his layup, he'd lost a few pounds, but nothing to be alarmed about. The doctors and nurses knew what it took to sustain a REV.

There was a disturbance at the other end of the mess decks. Two MPs—previously unnoticed by Zac until now—were arguing with a pair of Marines. Zac smiled. They were his kids: Jog and Bolt; Corporal Danny Gains and Staff Sergeant Manny Hernandez, the other two REVs aboard the *Olympus*.

While he was leaving the mess decks, Captain Keller eventually joined the discussion/debate before giving the junior REVs permission to join Zac at the table. Interaction between REVs was closely regulated and monitored. With just the slightest elevation in residual NT-4, the beasts in the men could come out, sometimes pitting man-against-man in an instinctive duel for animal supremacy. This didn't happen often, but when it did, it wasn't pretty.

The two men were none too happy when they slipped onto the bench opposite Zac.

"Idiots," said Jog, looking back at the guards. "I guess no one told them the mixture has been tweaked. We don't go all Alpha Male anymore."

Zac thought about growling at the young REV, but figured the nearby guards wouldn't see the humor in it.

He looked at Hernandez and the cast that was holding his right arm against his body, along with a variety of other bandages and angry cuts on his face.

"You should see the other guy," Manny said before Zac could ask about the injuries.

"How long has it been?"

"Seven days," Bolt replied. "I'm on the schedule fourteen days from now."

"Will you be ready?"

"Should be; are they letting you back in the rotation?"

Jog had cut half of Zac's remaining steak with a sharp plastic knife and was eating it with his fingers. He took note of the question. At the moment, Jog was the only cleared-for-duty REV onboard.

"Hell if I know. I only woke up a couple of hours ago, and no one has told me shit. You know Cross is on his way here?"

"Yeah, that's what we heard. So what's up? Why did they keep you under so long?"

"They couldn't get my levels down."

"Yeah, but why?" Jog asked between bites of the steak.

"That's what Cross is coming to find out, if he hasn't already."

"Well, if anyone can figure it out, he can," said Hernandez before changing the subject. "The kid goes out tomorrow."

Zac looked at the animated, handsome face of the twenty-three-year old REV. His eyes burned with fire in anticipation of a Run. It was like this for all REVs.

"Just a minor op," Danny said. "A platoon of Qwin are holed up in some lava tubes. You know how much I like lava tubes!"

And he did. Most REVs did. There weren't a lot of places for the aliens to hide so the body count was usually pretty high.

"I'll be in the command center during the Run," Zac informed him. "If they let me."

Hernandez leaned in closer and lowered his voice. "Zac, what's this about you stopping during the Run?"

Jog joined them in the huddle. "Yeah, and that you did it to lure in the Qwin?"

Zac sighed. "Yeah, apparently I did that."

"How…why?" Jog asked.

"Seemed like a good idea at the time."

Zac's comment was met by serious looks on the faces of the other two Marines.

"We're not supposed to have ideas during a Run, good or otherwise," said Hernandez.

"I know, and that's why everyone is watching me like a hawk."

NT-4 was a wonder drug, but it did have its side-effects. While under the influence, muscles strengthened, reactions quickened, and pain was subdued. For all intents and purposes, the subject became super-Human, capable of feats found only in ancient comic books and superhero movies.

Rev had first been developed as a steroid enhancement for athletes, supposedly nearly impossible to detect in its earlier forms. Unfortunately, the results couldn't be hidden. When the hundred-meters began being clocked at under eight seconds, monitoring groups knew something was up. It was a major scandal in its day.

But that didn't stop the military from carrying on the

research. It was one thing to cheat in sporting competitions. In war, there was no such thing as cheating. Opposing forces would use whatever means necessary to gain the upper hand, and Rev was one of those means.

At first they tried the drug on a vast number of soldiers and Marines, envisioning an entire army of super-Humans. The results were catastrophic. If the REVs weren't killing nearly everyone around them, they burned themselves out to the point where their hearts exploded. Rev sent blood pressure through the roof, often into the two-fifties, if not higher. The only thing keeping the subject alive was the increase capacity of the body thanks to the drug. Every system was elevated, including eyesight, memory, intelligence, capillary strength and endurance. But unchecked, the body couldn't handle the cascading effects.

With so many people being run through the program in the early days, researchers found that only certain individuals responded to the drug in the proper way. What was needed was a person who was susceptible, yet tolerant of its effects over the long run.

NOTES

"The subjects experience accelerated bodily functions in an uncontrolled, cascading effect. Recommend a pause of the program until an effective counter agent can be found. We're just killing too many damn people."

- Journal Entry, April 4, 2066, Dr. Clifford Slater

4

After the meal, Zac was allowed to return to his quarters instead of sickbay, yet the guards remained stationed outside, even with him locked in his room. This was SOP for the first week or so after being revived, but not after ninety-four days.

One of the perks of being a REV—and an E-7 gunnery sergeant—was that he got a private compartment aboard the carrier. It wasn't huge, but it was all his. There was a fold-away bunk on the starboard bulkhead, with a wardrobe and desk along the opposite wall. A small head was located in a side room, with a shower and toilet—his toilet. No matter how long he spent in the service, he could never get used to taking a crap in front a dozen bystanders, and them crapping next to him. It was just gross. And without the need to ration water on the huge starship—through the use of efficient recycling systems—he savored his long, hot showers in the privacy of his compartment.

Zac's only problem came from the fact that he was a social person. He enjoyed the company of others, especially his fellow

Marines. But as the years stacked up, and his legend grew, he found that most of them avoided his company, and notably within confined spaces. By then, stories were rampant of REVs flipping out and killing their comrades before they could be put down. These were men operating only on residual levels of the drug, but still subject to psychotic episodes. It was both a bane and a blessing that these incidents weren't accompanied by the full physical enhancements of the drug, such as ten-times the strength, quickness and durability of a normal person. These were only slightly-enhanced men going temporarily insane. They were easy to kill at that point and did relatively little damage on their own, even if the spontaneity of the episodes kept the stories alive.

Zac's irritated state didn't allow him to relax. The next five days would be torture, waiting for the general to arrive. And it was obvious he wouldn't be passing the time playing cards with any of his buddies.

However, Olivia Contreras was another matter.

He contacted her by shipboard link. She was off-duty and anxious to see him, but when she attempted to get permission from her senior command, they politely shut her down. They could talk by video link, but not in person, at least not until Zac was cleared for general interaction with the crew.

Olivia was an HMC1, a petty officer first-class Hospital Corpsman, assigned to the REV medical detail aboard the carrier. She was a dark-haired beauty from Southern California with twelve years in the Navy. As it was with most of the women aboard the ship, she had been instantly attracted to Zac on an instinctual level the first time she saw him. But she was also a pragmatist and understood better than most what she was experiencing. She chalked it up to animal attraction and left it at that.

But then during a rare forty-five day transit to the staging area around another ES world—when Zac had no Runs to go on or injuries to heal from—the two began to talk more and a bond developed. They hooked up a few times after that and the feelings grew stronger—until the time of Zac's next Run. Standing over his bedside, looking down at the battered and bloody comatose body, Olivia realized there was no future for the pair. She was heartbroken, and knew that if they got more serious, she'd have to relive these emotions every month or so with no end in sight.

They parted friends, with the occasional *benefit* thrown in when the time was right. But they kept their emotions in check, or at least they said they did.

Zac was stunned every time he saw Olivia, taken aback by her dark eyes, high cheekbones, full lips and radiant bronze hue of her skin. Even though there were tanning beds available aboard the carrier, most of the crew and troop compliment aboard were men, and they shunned the devices like the plague. But not so the three hundred females aboard, who monopolized the units. But a natural beauty like Olivia didn't need any help. She was in high demand everywhere she went.

Zac was ecstatic to see her on the video screen in his compartment, even if her expression was one of pouty frustration. "My god, you look great," he said with heartfelt sincerity.

"Thanks," she remarked automatically. "I'm just glad you're awake. I've been watching after you for three months, and now that you're up and moving around, they won't let me see you outside of sickbay."

Her fiery Latin temper was evident.

"Can you tell me any more about what happened?" Zac asked.

Frown lines appeared on her forehead. "There's so much security surrounding you at this point that I wouldn't be surprised if our conversation is being monitored, so I don't know what more I can say. As you've been told, no matter what we tried, your damn levels wouldn't come down. We pumped you so full of Twilight and RG-9 that any trace of NT-4 should have left your body, even the residual. As it is you're still at—"

A low-decibel buzz came over the speaker.

"See, I told you!" Olivia yelled.

"So no shop-talk?" Zac said with a pacifying smile.

A wicked grin, displaying starlet-white teeth, flashed back at him. "If they'd let us get together there wouldn't be much talking to censor!" she shouted for the benefit of the monitors. "So you see, it's better if you just let us screw. Anyone out there? Did you hear me?"

No one else came on the line.

"Well, since you can't give me any more details about my condition, maybe you can just sit there and let me stare at you."

"I'd be up for some video sex…if I didn't think the pervs in security were watching as well."

"At this point, I don't care."

Olivia expression changed from anger to sadness in a heartbeat. "I would, not knowing who had a copy. I get enough looks around the ship as it is."

"Looks of admiration, my dear."

"Try it from my side sometime…oh, I guess you have."

"When they let me stroll around the ship unattended, which isn't often. And honestly, when I'm all plastered up in casts and covered in bandages, that isn't much of a turn on."

Olivia smiled wickedly again. "Speak for yourself, big boy. Why do you think I became a corpsman? Broken and bloody men turn me on."

"You are one sick puppy, Ms. Contreras."

"Seriously," Olivia began, "I know we're not supposed to be

hooking up again, but after what you've been through, I think you deserve a good riding. I sure know I could use one."

"So you're not seeing anyone?"

"Just the usual suspects; a girl's gotta stay in practice for when she gets called up to the majors. So let's give it five days, until after Cross and his people take a look at you. After that all bets are off. And I have to say, this is the *cleanest* I've seen you since we met."

Zac knew what she meant. For most of the time they'd known each other, he was at some level of recovery from a Run. This was the most-healed he could remember being in the past fifteen years.

"You know in a way this could be a blessing," she said.

He nodded, understanding her meaning. It was beginning to look like his days as an active REV were coming to an end. Then depending on what was going on in his body, he may still have a chance to live out a somewhat normal life after the Marines, hopefully with Olivia at his side…as well as a whole cadre of monitors and medical professionals watching his every move.

The conversation lasted another few minutes before there was nothing left to say. They couldn't dream about the future, because they may not have one. And talk of the present was off-limits, while the past…well that was the past, and there was nothing they could do to change that.

For the past fifteen years, Zac Murphy knew exactly what he was and what he had to do. Now, as the video monitor turned black and reflected the lost look on his face, all he could see was the darkness surrounding his sad, gray features. Somehow it seemed appropriate.

NOTES

"Antaere, Qwin, they're all the same. They squeal like pigs when scared or hurt."

- Unknown soldier, ES-5

5

The next morning, after a heavy breakfast in his secluded corner of the mess decks, Zac was escorted to the operations command center overlooking the vast launch bay/staging area aboard the *Olympus*. The place was a buzz of activity as Corporal Danny Gains prepared for his Run.

Zac waved down at his young protégé and the still-healing Manny Hernandez down on the main deck. Jog was then placed into the EC and strapped in, before the canopy was locked into place.

Captain Keller was there, too, just as he'd been for Zac's last Run. The strange thing, to Zac it seemed like only yesterday, and from his perspective, it was; for the others, this was just another day on the job.

Zac surveyed the screens before him. As the senior REV aboard, he was an integral part of the operation. He would monitor Jog's vitals, scan the local surroundings and make operational adjustments if necessary…and possible. There was only so much outsiders could do to influence a Run. Subtle subliminal suggestions could be fed to the REV, but there was no guarantee they'd be noticed or obeyed.

REVs were the ultimate chase animals. About the only diversion from a basic wind-him-up-and-let-him-go strategy was when a REV would have to decide which group of aliens to follow if they split up. That usually came down to which group was larger. And then he was off again on his Run.

That's what made Zac's pretending to be Twilighted such a novelty. No one had ever done that before.

Zac would also have operational input regarding the deployment of the support troops, if not actual control. This included advising the Recovery Unit under Captain Keller's on-planet command, as well as the trailing infantry. As the most-senior REV in the Corps, his suggestions were respected. He'd seen more action than any of the officers or enlisted of higher rank— anywhere. They would be foolish not to accept his input.

Displayed on a screen was a schematic of the lava tube complex the aliens were hiding in. They were back at ES-8 but Zac didn't recognize the location. After a quick check, he found this operational sector was near the north polar region. The Marines of the main assault force were dressed in winter camo and all puffed out like snowmen—snowmen with deadly M-101 assault rifles, as well as an assortment of other deadly gear fastened to their uniforms.

The main lava tube ran under the surface of a large, extinct shield volcano. A section of the roof had collapsed, giving access to the underground labyrinth. The Qwin were about a klick from the opening, north along the main tube. There were other side tubes, but the heat signatures showed the major concentration along the main tunnel. There were about four hundred aliens all clustered within a thousand foot section.

Unlike Zac's last landing, Jog's EC would land within a few

feet of the craggy, black crusted opening and not shoot him out. A few Qwin were stationed as lookouts; more would come before Danny could make it to the ground.

The Qwin had eyes on the *Olympus*, just as the Humans had eyes on the Antaere ships nearby. As soon as the EC shot from the side of the ship, the aliens would go on alert. A few minutes later, they would identify the likely target and defensive measures would begin. On the ground, more troops would be moved toward the opening.

What the Qwin wouldn't know at this point is whether or not the assault would be led by a REV. Half of the recent operations had been traditional, with no REV involved, which was unusual. This was a result of Zac being out of the rotation. The Marine's success rate during these non-REV assaults was an impressive eighty-percent, although the casualties were high, higher than with a REV leading the way.

And now the Qwin were making a determined stand on ES-8, refusing to leave one of their most-settled worlds. Counting attacks initiated from both sides, the result so far was a stalemate. If Zac had stayed active, it would have been slightly in favor of the Humans.

Four hundred was a small contingent of Qwin, but they were operating an elaborate communications center from underground. Comms from orbit could be easily blocked by intercept satellites. Taking out the land-based center would leave the aliens in the dark over a quarter of the planet, at least until new links could be established. By then more Earth troops would be on the surface and taking up fortifying positions. Eventually the Qwin would abandon the planet, at least temporarily. Unfortunately, the aliens never permanently surrendered a position. Their religion wouldn't allow it.

For the Antaere, it was all about securing worshippers for their Universal Order. On every ES world, they built elaborate Temples dedicated to the yellow sun. They conveniently ignored the fact that there are *billions* of yellow suns in the galaxy, concentrating instead on only those with Antara-like worlds. Upon landing on a new world, they would tell the natives how special they were because of the unique nature of their existence. They were now part of a great Universal Order, of which the Antaere were the guardians. And all the natives had to do to be included was to obey the Antaere.

Recently, the Humans had upset the well-laid plans of the aliens to the point they were less concerned about the welfare of their followers than with simply killing every Human they could. Not surprising, that was exactly the same philosophy practiced by the Humans.

"Thirty seconds to initial boost, three minutes to drop," Zac heard Capt. Keller say to Jog over the comm, an all-too familiar litany from the team commander.

"Watch my six, gunny," the young REV said to Zac through the comm.

"Will do, squirt. Now just relax and enjoy the ride. The inflight movie today is *Athena's Eyes* starring the vivacious Jennifer Lawrence."

"I thought she died forty years ago?"

"Movie stars don't die these days, Jog. They live on in digital. You should know that."

"I do and I don't care. She's still hot!"

"And just think, they can make her do anything they want."

"Dammit, gunny, now you have me thinking of things other than the mission…."

His voice trailed off as the first of the pre-drugs was administered.

"He's gone," said Manny Hernandez. "He should have some nice dreams thanks to you, Zac."

"In a few minutes the thrill of killing aliens will replace any wet dreams he has about a long-dead movie star."

Hernandez laughed. "Damn straight. We sure are a strange bunch, aren't we, gunny?"

"No argument there. Drop in forty-five. Good luck Captain Keller."

"Same to you," said the Marine officer. "Stay in touch."

"Yes sir."

The first part of the operation went off like clockwork. Jog landed fifty meters from the long, narrow crack in the black surface of the shield volcano and immediately jumped into the abyss, landing sixty feet down on the worn floor of the lava tube.

The Qwin had brought up another twenty troops from the main cluster. Jog's descent in a solitary pod had tipped off the aliens that this *was* a REV landing, so the Qwin near the entrance didn't put up much of a fight. They retreated into the dark, basalt-lined tunnel, trying to get a jump ahead of the speeding REV. Half of them survived to meet up with the first fortified line of defense.

The aliens had pulled down the sides of the tunnel on the left and right and were hiding behind piles of fallen obsidian rock. Zac watched the four cameras on Jog's battle collar and saw his protégé execute a neat maneuver that impressed even him. Danny literally ran up one side of the lava tube, blasted the aliens on the right, and then performed a somersault and landed behind the Qwin on the left. None of the aliens at this location survived to tell the tale of the deadly acrobatic move.

That still left over three hundred Qwin still in the tunnel. They ran to a fork in the lava tube and separated. In most circumstances this wouldn't have been a problem. In a city or a building complex, the road grid could be tracked and the supporting Marines sent to intercept. The REV wasn't expected to do *all* the work, just most of it. But in a complex of underground tunnels, each tube was often a separate channel unto itself and may never meet up with the main tube again.

Jog paused, his supercharged brain scanning the fleeing aliens, before deciding that the group to the left was the larger. He sprinted after them.

Zac hurriedly pulled up the scans of this new section of lava tube. All he had were satellite soundings, so the details weren't well-defined. The tube was narrower here, which was fine for the REV, but it would limit the access for the recovery team and the trailing Marines.

Capt. Keller and Col. Owens—the same officer duo who supported Zac on his last Run—were struggling to keep up. The second group of Qwin who had separated from the main force was back and harassing the Marines on their right flank. The Humans had to duck for cover every few feet and return fire.

A squad of Marines moved past the others and took up a more permanent position within the main tube, providing cover for the rest of the force. Keller ordered his men forward, and once in the clear, they raced in Jog's direction ahead of the main Marine contingent. It was nearing the ten minute mark and they were thirty seconds behind their REV.

Zac studied a screen as flashes from Jog's pulse rifle lit up the dimly lit tunnel. Alien bodies were everywhere; Jog was in the zone and nearing the end of his Run.

Just then, Zac noticed something strange about the Qwin's return fire. It wasn't aimed at Jog. It took him a moment to realize the truth. They were shooting at the ceiling of the tube, directly above Jog.

Zac brought his microphone close to his mouth and began to chant softly: "Roof, roof, roof…"

The transducer wires leading into Jog's head would relay the soft, constant message into the REV's brain. It would register within the deep, subliminal recesses of his mind, giving the juiced up warrior a suggestion, a hint, something to consider.

After a few seconds Zac noticed the angle of Jog's camera shift upwards. He directed his fire at the top of a narrow part of the tunnel, above where most of the Qwin were hiding. Black rock began to rain down on the aliens, even as Zac could see the same shower of stone falling from the ceiling from Jog's point of view. It was a race to see who could bring down the ceiling first.

Jog lost.

Since there was no such thing as retreat for a REV, Danny was still in the chamber when the roof fell in over him. He was knocked to the floor and buried by a huge pile of black volcanic rock. For a normal Human, this would have been fatal. But not for a REV. Jog, pressed, twisted and screamed, using his incredible strength, toughness of his NT-4-enchanced skin and remaining battle armor to lift the boulders from his body. They tumbled to the side as Jog struggled to get to his feet.

He came out of the pile with his weapon firing, cutting down a line of aliens who had begun to close in on the pile of rock.

Zac checked Keller's position. He was almost to the small lava chamber with his recovery team. Two squads of Marines were only steps behind.

Ten minutes, fourteen seconds into the Run. A look at Jog's vitals showed that he was nearing Twilight time. The battle computer would make the final call.

"Dammit!" Zac heard Keller yell out over a rumbling through the speakers.

"Captain?"

"The tunnel just gave way in front of us! We're cut off from Gains."

Zac checked his screen. Jog was still firing, but he wasn't advancing. Detectors on his battle armor reported a crushed right leg and a foot lodged within the boulders. Jog was trapped and his support cut off.

It was eleven minutes into the Run and the young REV would be Twilighted any second. With no backup, he would be ripped to shreds by the aliens.

Zac keyed in the destruct code. Techs to either side of him saw his hand move on the console and knew what he was doing. No one protested. They were just glad it wasn't them making the call.

With only the slightest hesitation, Zac pressed the execute button.

The scene in the lava chamber flared only briefly before the screen went black.

Zac leaned back in the chair and sighed. He felt a moment of loss and sadness, not from what he'd done, but for the loss of a friend and colleague. Although Jog didn't have the authority to do to what Zac had just done—someone of higher rank would have made the call—he was sure the young REV would done the same for him.

"What was that?" Keller yelled through the comm. "Did you—"

"Yessir," Zac interrupted. "Cut off, injured and moments from Twilight. I made the call."

There was silence on the line for a few tense seconds.

"I concur. Action approved," said Captain Keller. "Now,

where are the rest of those yellow-skinned bastards? We may as well try to get some payback while were still in the shit."

For a *minor* op, it had been costly. Eventually, all the Qwin were killed and the comm station destroyed, but of the ninety deploying Marines, thirty had been killed and seventeen wounded. Even four from Keller's medical team had been injured after they entered the active fight to clear the tunnels.

Eventually, a path was found through the main tunnel back to the chamber were Jog had died, but as expected, there was nothing to recover, not even a dog-tag. The explosion wasn't large, just enough to take out the REV and any alien troops within a fifteen foot circle.

There had been four hundred Qwin in the tunnels; Jog was given credit for killing three hundred nine of them. That may have been generous, but no one complained. It went into his service record and was added to his total on a wall back on Earth honoring all the REV dead in this war.

This was Zac's eighteenth *Final Call*. As a senior REV, it wouldn't be his last.

NOTES

Observable acceleration in healing is noted in all subjects on the NT-3a regimen. This was not expected, yet welcome. This phenomenon coincides with the trace amounts retained in the tissue. The R-class counter-agent appears to help in reducing levels following full activation. Still, too many deaths. My new assistant has been assigned to study the residual effect. He is a strange one.

- Journal Entry, Dec. 15, 2069, Dr. Clifford Slater

6

Three days later Zac met up with Manny Hernandez coming down a wide corridor within Officer's Country aboard the starship, still sporting the white cast over his left arm. The cuts on his face had healed to just dull red lines on his dark skin, thanks in part to the healing power of the residual REV in his system. His arm would take only three weeks to heal completely.

Zac's escorting guards numbered only two this time, not because their ranks had been reduced, but because there would be plenty of others already on station for the upcoming meeting.

While still twenty feet from the meeting room, Zac's enhanced hearing picked up the ranting of a deep-voiced man echoing off the walls.

"What the hell is happening to your unit, Captain Keller? First one of your REVs goes rogue during a Run, then another gets his ass shot up. And to top it off, the rogue REV then gives the command to blow up another of his team. Right now, this battle-carrier doesn't have a single operational REV onboard. That's unacceptable."

"We're expediting another trio from Earth," said another voice in the room. "ETA, fourteen days."

"In the meantime, the fucking Qwin are making the strongest push they ever have for an ES planet right here on number eight. That means a lot more Marines are going to die before we can get some REVs out in front."

"REV's are Marines, too, general."

Zac recognized the voice as that of Arnie Patel. He could imagine the look he was getting from the general, even if no words could be heard. Zac rushed ahead to the door, hoping to run interference for his friend.

One of the two guards at the door rapped strongly.

"Enter!" said the gruff voice of General Simon 'Mad-Dog' McCabe.

The guard opened the door and Zac and Manny entered. They stepped up to the too-tall officer and stood ridged at attention.

"Sir, Gunnery Sergeant Murphy and Staff Sergeant Hernandez reporting as ordered."

The General's face was flush from anger. He studied the two men before him and then nodded. "At ease, gentlemen. Please take seats at the table."

As Zac moved around to the other side of the long, mahogany-topped table, he noticed it was bolted to the floor, as were the two chairs on his side of the table. Those on the other side were freestanding and occupied by five people, not counting the towering senior officer, while another four men stood along the far bulkhead—along with four Marine guards. It seemed no one was taking chances with the two REVs in the room, even if one was in a cast.

Zac was disappointed to see that Olivia wasn't with Patel. She said she'd try to be present, but it looked as though the moratorium on them meeting face-to-face was still on.

Zac's attention shifted when the general sat down across from him. McCabe was six-foot-six, which was far too tall for the passage- and doorways aboard a battle-carrier. He began his career with the infantry, fighting the Qwin in the early days on alien worlds with plenty of headroom. As he advanced through rank, however, more of his time was spent aboard starships. His nickname of *mad-dog* came not so much from his command style, but rather from the frequent temper tantrums he'd exhibit after banging his head into yet another hatchway or overhead. At six-foot-two, Zac had met his share of hatchways as well, but nothing like the irascible officer now glaring at him from across the table.

"Care to fill me in about the events of three days past, gunny?" the general commanded.

"Sir," Captain Keller said. "I approved the decision—"

"Retroactively, captain," McCabe barked.

"Sir, ordering the death of a fellow REV is not something I do lightly," Zac said. He didn't feel like he had to explain himself, but was being asked to do so. "Corporal Gains was already dead in my opinion. I only wished to make his death count for a little more by taking a few extra Qwin with him."

McCabe pursed his lips. "I understand that, gunny. I know it wasn't an easy decision, but one that was necessary. I'm just frustrated with the loss of a good REV. When added to the other deficiencies of your team, I'm thinking about the loss of Marine's lives that will result from those deficiencies. I apologize for my outburst. It wasn't personal."

"General, I feel the same. And in light of the Qwin offensive on ES-8, I would like to get operational as soon as possible."

McCabe looked over at a tall, slender man in summer khakis, sporting a full head of silver-gray hair that was much too long for a combat Marine. "Dr. Cross and I arrived about the same time aboard the *Olympus*, but from separate directions. He hasn't briefed me on his findings." He frowned at the scientist. "He seems to be making a mystery out of it."

Colonel David Cross and Zac had met three times in the past, the first being fifteen years ago during the workup to graduation from REV training. Zac was amazed to see that the man appeared to have aged very little. He was still lean and ruggedly handsome. Only the hair hinted at his true age of fifty-six. As the lead scientist and inheritor of the NT-4 work done by the famous Doctor Clifford Slater, he would make a perfect recruiting poster for the program, if he were a REV. Instead, he was a geek in a lab coat, constantly working to improve his magic elixir.

Cross smiled. "I apologize, general. It was not my intention to be secretive, but we were still refining our datasets when we left Earth. Twenty-eight days in transit meant we still had a lot of work to do on the way here. It was either work along the way or postpone the announcement."

"What announcement?" asked both Zac and Dr. Patel in unison.

Cross looked around the room. "I see that very few here have an in-depth understanding of NT-4 and the program surrounding its use, so I would like to take a moment to set the stage for what I will say later. It will add context to the announcement. Do I have your permission, general?"

"It took me two weeks to get here, doctor. And now that I am, you have a captive audience. But don't take too long or make it too boring."

Zac nodded to himself. That sounded like something he might say. Maybe the general wasn't so bad after all....

Doctor Cross focused his attention on Zac.

"I must say, Sergeant Murphy, I feel like we're old friends, and I suspect you wouldn't be surprised to learn that we have a whole unit back at the Center devoted to you, and you alone."

"I figured that after all these years someone had to take notice."

"And we have. It's a little known fact, but we collect data on every REV and every Run they take. This data is then categorized and sorted to rate each operative based on this information. Needless to say, you are far and away the top REV in the program."

"Excuse me, sir, but what does that mean exactly?" Zac asked, growing weary of the show taking place. "I'm juiced up and pointed in a direction. I have no control over what I do and cannot consciously use any special skills I may have. I kill aliens by the truckload and only survive because of the toughness of my REV-enhanced skin, my strength and heightened senses. I'm like every other REV in that regard. So how do I rate higher than Sergeant Hernandez, for example?"

"That's a fair question, gunny," said Dr. Cross. "And as I continue with my presentation, I hope to answer it. May I?"

The guy sure is a polite bastard, Zac thought.

"Please, sir, continue."

"As I was saying, as you continued on your phenomenal tenure as a REV, we began to take note and assigned a team of specialists to assess your condition and accomplishments. We needed to answer two questions. One: Are you unique in your abilities and longevity. And two: Are you a precursor to what all long-term NT-4 users will become? The data was stacking up, and honestly, if this recent event hadn't occurred, I was getting ready to pull you from the field and bring you back to Earth for more study."

"What did you find?" asked Dr. Arnie Patel.

"Up to a month ago, all we could definitively say was that Zac is unique."

"A month?" said Captain Keller. "That was well after the Run."

"Yes it was, captain," Cross said, seeming to enjoy the game of suspense he was playing. "Let me summarize what happened during and after the Run, and then attempt to link the cause and effect of both.

"Gunnery Sergeant Murphy performed remarkably well during the Run, so much so that he exceeded record kill numbers, as well as distance penetrated into enemy territory. That alone would have got our attention, especially since this was accomplished by the most-senior REV in the program. One would think that as a person grows older, and the more wear and tear the body sustains, abilities would diminish over time. But not so for our indestructible gunnery sergeant. All our data showed an *increase* in ability and a strengthening of his systems over the past several Runs. Normally, we would have accepted this information on face value, believing that long-term use of NT-4 would cause others to achieve the same results. But that doesn't seem to be happening. Sergeant Murphy is the exception, not the rule."

Cross stopped and turned to an assistant leaning against the wall behind him. The man handed him a stack of thin datapads. Cross passed them out around the table, including to Zac and Manny. They activated automatically as Cross began to scan through the pages.

"Let me go over some basic data about NT-4, some of which you may already know but will be essential as I go forward." He highlighted a section on the datapad.

"NT-4 is often referred to as a super drug, something able

to turn ordinary men into super men. Unfortunately, that is not the case. All NT-4 does is trigger the body to do what it does naturally, but at much higher levels and efficiency. We call this the *cascading effect*. When even a small trace of the drug is introduced into the body, this cascading begins. The problem we found in the early days was that once the cascading began there was no way to stop it. Even if no additional NT-4 was introduced, the body continued to spiral out of control. In the days before Twilight, I have watched men literally explode from the pressure building up inside. And even with Twilight—along with its cousin RD-9—the body couldn't survive the stresses placed upon it. It was later discovered that a massive dose of NT-4 would help stabilize the cascading effect, but only for a period of ten to twelve minutes. After that, no amount of NT-4—or even Twilight—would help. The subject would continue to cascade, resulting in a very messy death. That is why an *activated* REV can only operate for a finite period, with twelve minutes being the absolute maximum safe duration."

He paused to look at Zac before returning to the datapad.

"The Human body is an amazing thing, and will do all it can to protect itself. That's why it retains a certain amount of residual NT-4. Yes, gentlemen, we did *not* design the drug to remain in the body in residual amounts. This is something the body does on its own. Every person who takes NT-4 remains operating at an elevated level, even when not activated. This increases certain bodily functions, which for a normal person, would result in either an embolism, cardiac arrest or other critical malady. The only thing keeping a REV's body from burning up is the residual amount of NT-4 in the system.

"And that is why NT-4 doesn't make the REV super Human. What it does is allow the body to *survive* the cascading effects, either over the short-term for an activated REV, or longer while in a passive state.

"Now let me tell you about Sergeant Murphy."

He flipped the page on the screen and Zac was surprised to see a picture from his enlistment profile. He hadn't seen it for a long time, and the marked difference in the shape of his face was startling. *Damn, I was a gangly-looking kid.*

"A passive REV has an average residual NT-4 in his system of approximately seven percent. This varies between individuals, based upon their time in the system and number of activations they've undergone. Because of his record-setting longevity, Zac carries a residual amount of ten-point-two percent." He held up his hand to head off any exclamations from the room, although no one seemed about to burst forth with questions. Instead, they appeared anxious for Cross to get to the point.

The doctor continued: "This is a normal level for him, and doesn't mean he's continually on the verge of spontaneously cascading. This is just the amount of NT-4 his body has determined it needs to survive his increased physiological activity."

Cross smiled and looked around the room. "However, it does mean our Sergeant Murphy is about forty percent stronger than your average REV, with senses proportionally more acute, even when not activated. So watch what you say around him gentlemen; he has hearing more sensitive than a dog's."

No one in the room was in the mood for Cross's lecture hall humor, especially not Zac. The scientist was taking far too long getting to the point.

When no one even smiled, Cross pursed his lips and continued in earnest. "During the Run in question, Sergeant Murphy also exhibited behavior never before seen in a REV. When he pretended to be Twilighted, he showed forethought, planning and conscious execution of the plan, brought about by a rational assessment of the battle taking place. This placed him within the action and consciously aware of it. Not only that, but he remained unmoving on the ground for seventeen seconds. Gentlemen, imagine drinking a hundred cups of coffee and then being asked to lie on the floor, perfectly still. You couldn't do it, not even for five seconds. Now multiply that by a hundred, and you have the electric energy coursing through an activated REV. Zac did just that. And then he stood up and resumed the fight.

"Needless to say, we had a lot of additional questions about our super REV after that. But it was when he was brought back aboard the *Olympus*—and Dr. Patel and his staff had trouble bring the NT-4 levels down in his system—that I began to suspect there was something inhibiting the effectiveness of the diluting drugs, and it wasn't my NT-4."

"A contaminant of some kind?" Arnie asked. "We suspected that, too, but couldn't isolate anything abnormal."

"That's because you weren't looking in the right place. You were looking for a foreign contaminant, when you should have been looking at the NT-4 itself."

"But you just said NT-4 wasn't the cause."

"It wasn't. The reason Zac was able to do what he did, and why it took you and your team three months to get his levels down, is because Sergeant Murphy has begun to produce a *natural* form of NT-4."

Now the room did explode in a cacophony of questions and protests, with the most prominent words heard above the din being *how* and *why*. Cross didn't attempt to calm the outbursts, instead reveling in the wake of his nuclear statement.

It was Zac who brought the people in the room back to their senses.

"Bullshit!" he yelled out, adding 'sir' a moment later just to keep things copasetic. "How does a body start producing something it never has before? It takes millions of years of evolution to change a system. It doesn't happen in just a few years."

"I beg to differ with you, sergeant, but the accepted consensus is that evolution is not a straight-line affair, but rather moves in fits and starts as the need arises. Darwin showed how over a relative few generations, the shape of bird's beaks could change, and claws become webbed. For a long time, humanity has lived within a fairly stable environment, so the need for radical change hasn't been necessary—"

"Excuse me, colonel," General McCabe interrupted. "I don't think we need a biology lesson at this point. Could we concentrate on Sergeant Murphy? Your claim is startling. I'm going to need some proof of what you say."

Cross lifted his hands toward Zac. "There it is, general. After ninety days without a boost, Sergeant Murphy is still alive."

"He had an abundance of NT-4 still in his system long after the Run," Arnie Patel countered. "It allowed his system to survive the stresses longer than normal."

"Have you checked his residual recently?" Cross asked.

Patel looked defeated. "It's at eighteen percent."

Another murmur spread throughout the room. Even Manny looked at Zac and said, "Damn!"

"That was as low as we could get him," Patel said in his defense. "He showed no signs of cascading, so I decided to revive him."

"And there has been no appreciative cascading since," Cross reported. "Yet we both know a REV with eighteen percent NT-4 would be well on his way to full activation. In fact, for Zac, anything over eleven percent would trigger him. So why has he not?"

"Is this just a theory of yours, doctor, so you can explain something you don't understand?" asked General McCabe.

"No sir. During the trip out here, we were able to isolate the hormone and map—at least partially—the process involved. But rest assured, general, Zac's body is doing what I say."

Cross leaned back in his chair and placed his hands on the table. "At this point, however, I need to clarify a few points. First: Zac is not producing NT-4, but rather something close to it. His body has somehow determined the proper combination of hormones, proteins and other ingredients to mimic the effects of the drug. And it does blend rather nicely with the synthetic, making it extremely difficult to detect."

"So why isn't he going berserk?" asked Captain Keller.

Zac looked at his squad leader and frowned. He didn't like the way they were talking about him as if he wasn't there, especially when using words like *berserk*.

"That's something we need to find out," said Cross. "It's evident that the natural form of NT-4 doesn't enhance the synthetic, but somehow controls it."

"Dilutes it?" Patel asked.

"Not necessarily. If that were the case I don't think Sergeant Murphy would have activated the last time. And even after all this time, he is still retaining a residual amount of the synthetic."

"Assuming what you say is true," began General McCabe, obviously still not sold on the concept, "what does this mean for the viability of the REV program?"

"I'm not sure, general. You have to understand it was only about forty days ago that I even began to suspect some outside influence was affecting the NT-4 in Zac's system. There is still a lot of research to do."

"And what does this mean for me?" Zac asked. His mind was in turmoil, as was his future. "Am I out of the program…out of the Marines?"

"I can't say, sergeant. With this new development, we have

no idea what it will take to activate you, or if it's even possible. And if so, then how much Twilight do we administer to counter the effects? In addition, do you retain control during a Run—"

"Which would be extremely dangerous," said Col. Diamond, speaking for the first time.

"Excuse me, sir?" said Zac.

All eyes turned to the intelligence officer. The grim faces of the senior officers in the room told Zac that Diamond was about to voice what they were all thinking.

"Sergeant, do you have any idea how powerful you are when activated?"

Zac gnashed his teeth. Off course he did. He'd been a REV for fifteen fucking years. "Yeah, I'm pretty badass."

The officer glared back at Zac. "That you are. But you also have to admit you've never actually *felt* yourself being activated. When you cascade, you lose all sense of physical awareness. Sure, your mind records the images of the Run, but your memory doesn't recall how it *feels*. It's estimated you gain ten times the strength of a normal Marine, along with all other related body functions. That's incredible."

"Yes it is…sir."

"You also are obedient, to a degree."

Zac's temper flared. He didn't know if the officer was intentionally trying to provoke him, but he was.

Diamond continued. "The way it works now is we point you in a direction and you more-or-less obey. Now imagine you arbitrarily decide to turn around and go back the way you came… because *you* made the decision to do so. You'd run smack dab into your own troops. What would you do then?"

"Since *I* made the decision to turn around, *I* would probable decide not to kill my fellow Marines."

"Can you say that for certain, sergeant? If not, then what are we supposed to do with you?"

"We're talking in hypotheticals here," Arnie Patel said, trying to put the conversation in perspective.

"Doctor Patel is correct," said David Cross. "That's why we need to run some test...experiments, really."

"Experiments?"

"Yes, sergeant. We need to study the effects of this natural version of NT-4 in combination with the synthetic. We need to test dosages and then counters to the dosage. The amount you produce naturally is relatively low compared to a full combat dose, but it's omnipresent. We also need to know if we can control its production, possibly with medication. I hope you realize what a significant event this is. If we find that continued use of NT-4 over extended periods can create this condition in others, then we need to plan for it."

The doctor's statement was a more subtle reiteration of what Diamond just said: We can't have a bunch of people making Rev on their own. That would be far too dangerous...and unpredictable.

"Zac, do we have your permission to run the tests?"

Zac was a Marine; he knew they didn't need his permission to do the testing, but it would be better if he volunteered. He firmed his resolve. He was a Marine first and foremost, and he wanted to stay one. If finding the answers—and possibly a cure—for his condition would make that possible, he wouldn't stand in the way.

"Of course, sir, I'm at your disposal." He regretted the last word in the sentence. If it came down to it, the Corps wouldn't hesitate to *dispose* of him if need be.

NOTES

Dr. Cross has reported an increasing residual in subjects with six or more activations. This coincides with the increase in metabolism observable in all longer-term participants. I am ready to begin trials on NT-3b. This appears to be a more stable form of the drug. We shall see.

- Journal Entry, Feb. 17, 2070, Dr. Clifford Slater

7

The first of the tests was scheduled for oh-ten hundred the next morning. Before leaving the meeting in the wardroom, Dr. Cross gave Zac a powerful, fast-acting laxative and a sleeping pill. The laxative worked; the sleeping pill didn't.

When he arrived in MedLab the next morning, the place was packed with lab coats, khakis and armed guards. It seemed everyone wanted to be witness to the Zac Murphy Show. Even the ship's captain was present. In the year he'd been aboard the *Olympus*, Zac only seen the man a dozen times before. Now he stood on the other side of the viewing window next to General McCabe. From his expression, Zac got the impression he was there to see just how dangerous Zac was to his ship and crew. He didn't fault the man for his concern.

Zac was stripped to the waist and placed in a reinforced hospital bed. He was familiar with the set up. When not scheduled for a Run, REVs were required to get periodic maintenance boosts of NT-4 to sustain their residual levels. They would be strapped into a bed like this and fired up with a combat dose of the drug. But rather than letting the ten-to-twelve minute cascading period run, Twilight would be administered immediately. Since it happened so fast, and without the accompanying injuries sustained during a Run, the REV would be released from the hospital within a couple of days, with no lasting effects, except for a tiny boost in residual.

But now Zac bit his bottom lip when the technicians closed the restraints over his arms and legs, and the IV's were plugged into his veins. They assured him all the precautions were for his protection, yet everyone left the room and electronically locked the door behind them.

Through the large observation window, Zac saw the officers and attendants hover over the shoulders of the medical team seated at a console in the control room. Armed guards were stationed in the foyer outside Zac's room. He counted four armed with CQC-barreled M-101s. During maintenance sessions, one was always on station—just in case—yet armed with tranq darts, not deadly assault weapons.

Zac didn't know exactly what was about to happen, but he suspected the doctors first needed to test his activation level of NT-4 in conjunction with his natural Rev. He couldn't remember the last time a REV was brought to full activation within a closed environment...and left that way. It would be like setting off a bomb.

He was also hoping they had plenty of Twilight around in case his body cascaded off the edge. And what about the passage of time? Would it be another three months before he awoke again...if ever? In fact, the doctors may just play with his body until it burned out, while they gained *valuable insight* into this new wrinkle in the REV Program?

In a very real sense, Zac felt like he was sitting in an electric chair, breathing his last conscious breath.

"Okay, Zac, we're going to start in a few seconds," said Arnie Patel through the intercom. "Try to relax."

"That's easy for you to say."

Arnie didn't respond.

Dr. Cross leaned over to the microphone. "Gunny, we're going to introduce the NT-4 gradually, and not in a full combat boost like you're used to."

Zac laughed. No one ever got used to being suddenly changed from a normal person into a crazed killing monster. That's why the primal scream was a signature of his kind.

Zac was shocked by the significance of that last thought: *His kind*. With the production of naturally-occurring Rev, was he becoming something different, something more than Human… or maybe less? Sure, the enhanced physical capacities of a REV were beyond normal. But so was the rage. When activated, he was more an animal than a man. Even if he was turning into something different could it be allowed to survive?

Zac noticed the effects of NT-4 being introduced into his system for the first time in his life. Although under normal operations, the primal scream was the signal of the drug's introduction, REVs never remembered the outburst. Only recordings provided evidence to them that it occurred. Although masculine bravado called for the REV to exhibit pride in the savage battle cry, inside they felt embarrassed by the loss of control it signified. With so many people watching, Zac hoped he wouldn't experience the same thing.

But now he began to concentrate more on the moment, worrying less about what others may think. He was experiencing something completely foreign to him. Gone was the sudden surge of strength and energy, replaced now by a strange sensation of well-being. His muscles tensed and his senses began working at a heightened level. The room became brighter, more detailed, and he could hear the conversation in the other room even without the microphone. There was a strong odor of bleach and alcohol, and the sheet under his body felt soft and warm.

His heart rate increased as his blood pressure approached two-hundred over one-forty. The longer he stayed on the drug, the higher it would go.

Zac wasn't sure how much of the dose was in his system. He could feel an incredible power in his body and clarity of mind. Even after fifteen years as a REV, this was a new experience for him. He laughed out loud. This was incredible…if annoying. He was growing restless. He wished they would get on with the test.

"Sergeant, how do you feel? Can you talk to us?" It was Dr. Cross on the intercom.

"I feel fine," Zac snapped. "How far along am I?" His jaw began to involuntarily slip back and forth, grinding his teeth. But he didn't care.

The doctors in the control room looked at each other, confused. Cross spoke into the microphone again. "Are you saying you don't feel anything?"

Zac took several deep breaths to regain his composure. It seemed everything Cross said made him mad. "Yeah, I feel it. It's just…different."

"In what way?"

Zac gnashed his teeth. Dammit, he just said it was *different*.

"I don't know. Fuck! I have nothing to compare it too."

"He shouldn't be able to talk, let alone reason." It was the voice of Arnie Patel. Zac had never noticed how annoyingly high-pitched it was….

Patel looked up at General McCabe. Zac could hear the

general's voice through the speaker—or through the window—he couldn't tell which. "Increase by twenty percent."

"That's beyond combat dose," Arnie Patel protested.

"Just do it…slowly. We need to know his limits. This is not what we expected."

"He's cascading, general, but in a unique way," Dr. Cross reported. "We need to stop now and study the data. The natural NT-4 is moderating the synthetic somehow. This is significant."

"What are his vitals?"

"They're in the green, but that's not the point," said Cross.

"Then he's in no danger," McCabe said.

"We don't know that for sure."

"Just do it, colonel."

There was tense silence in the control room before Cross shook his head and returned his attention to the console. "Yes sir."

Zac felt even more warmth spread throughout his body. The sensation of euphoria was now mixed with the growing frustration, creating a dichotomy of emotions. Thoughts became jumbled, more frantic; a conflict between the sane man and the insane killer.

He began to struggle against his restraints. He couldn't just lie here, not any longer. He needed…to move.

The restraints around his ankles and wrists were the standard design used to secure REVs during maintenance boosts. No one had had the time or forethought to change them for Zac's test. Even then, they were incredibly strong and unbreakable. Unfortunately, the connecting structure of the bed wasn't as strong.

As Zac pulled, the base of the bed began to bend upward,

forming a long cradle for his body in the mattress. The leg posts were the first to give way, followed moments later by the arms. Zac sprang to his feet, his limbs still wrapped in the restraints, but now with half the bed's metal rods dangling from them.

Through a small window in the door, he saw the guards move into position. Zac ran toward the door, crashing his rock-hard body into the metal panel. It buckled but didn't break. He stepped back and tried it again, this time letting out the signature primal scream.

The door fell outward, landing on top of two of the guards. Another had his weapon aimed at Zac. The rifle discharged and the high-caliber bullet hit his shoulder and passed through. Zac ignored the injury and continued running, dropping a shoulder into the guard who just shot him. He ran into an outer corridor just as another round ricocheted off the metal wall next to his head.

He heard yelling, orders to stop firing. Surveying the hallway, Zac spotted a group of people to his left, stunned into immobility. They angered him, but not enough for him to attack. He turned to the right and began running, glancing back as others entered from the MedLab. Each of these men had handguns. But they weren't normal weapons; instead injection guns with high-power darts tipped with thick needles. Several of the darts flew past his head, while others struck in the bare skin of his back. He was aware enough to know this probably wasn't Twilight, but something stronger, designed not to negate the NT-4 in his system but to simply knock him out.

Carrying even a larger dose of Rev than normal, Zac arrogantly ignored the darts even as his body began to feel the effects. He staggered and slipped on the blood pouring from the hole in his shoulder. Regaining his balance momentarily, he fell against the right side of the hallway then pushed off with his arms in anger. He should be able to keep his balance, but his legs were betraying him. He stumbled through a double door entry and into a much larger room filled with couches and chairs.

There was a scream as two women raced from the room through another doorway. Zac fell again, this time crashing headlong into a glass coffee table. His eyesight was obscured by something covering his face. He crawled forward, toward a person standing a few feet away.

Propping himself up with one arm, he wiped the blood from his face. For a brief moment he thought he saw his friend Manny Hernandez standing in front of him. He blinked hard and ran his hand across his face a second time so he could see. It *was* Manny. Zac reached out with his free hand.

"Manny…help!"

And then the strong fist of unconsciousness gripped him. Everything went black, and with it all the confusion and rage disappeared.

NOTES

Officials with the United Nations Doping in Sports subcommittee issued their final verdict today for the contestants charged with the use of the so-called 'Rev' drug in the last Olympics, stripping them of all medals and other awards, and banning each for life from participation in any sanctioned competitions.

- New York Times, Nov 6, 2052

8

Do you dream when you're dead?

That was Zac's question when he became aware of the phantom images in his mind. He didn't believe in an afterlife…but could he really be sure? Now he began to analyze his awareness. It was there, and he knew he had dreamed, but the mental constructs vanished quickly, replaced by a dull reality. He could feel his breathing. This definitely felt like living, which only confused him more.

He opened his eyes a little, assaulted by the glare of bright lights. His mouth felt like sandpaper, his lips cracked.

"Thank god," someone said from beyond his line of sight. "Now I won't have to change your stinking bedpans anymore."

He opened his eyes a little more and turned a stiff neck toward the sound. A young man in a green smock stood next to where he lay. Zac took a moment to survey where he was. He was in yet another bed in another hospital room, aware of the sores on his chest from the strap that ran across it, as well as the burning in his legs and wrists from the restraints clamped around them.

"Where…." He stopped speaking, overcome by the fiery pain in his throat.

"Don't try to speak, killer," said the young man. He poured water from a flask into a smaller cup and helped Zac moisten his lips and tongue before allowing him to down the rest of it. It was a combination of heaven and hell, as the water made its way down his throat.

"Where…am I?"

"Not sure where *you* are, but I've been in hell for these past few months. Now that you're awake you can take your own shits and showers. I swear, this is the most disgusting job I've ever had."

"Job…?"

The man shook his head.

"I'm one of three miserable souls assigned to keep your drooling body clean and nourished. You're not allowed to leave the bed, and you haven't in three months. You've just been a dead lump of sores and shit for all that time. You know, I didn't join the Navy so I could be your personal toilet paper. Hospital Corpsman sounded like a skate job. Bullshit. I'm doing my four and out. Screw this."

The orderly turned and left the room, even as Zac tried to call him back.

He relaxed his head against the pillow and stared at the ceiling. His senses were returning, and a few moments later he was to the point where he would be with the wake-up drugs after a dose of Twilight.

He was alive, healed from his injuries, and once again chained to a hospital bed. Some things never change.

Memories came to him, of the so-called experiment, his subsequent escape and being taken down by a barrage of tranquilizer darts. He could also vividly recall the face of Staff Sergeant Manny Hernandez after Zac called out to him. Beyond that…nothing.

Until now.

The corpsman said he'd been caring for Zac for three months. That was about right; the time it took for his body to purge enough of the synthetic Rev from his system to make him somewhat normal again. But the definition of *normal* had changed. What was normal to a man who was spitting natural Rev into his system on a regular basis?

And then there were the restraints, and the obvious time he'd worn them. It didn't take a genius to figure out something had changed. He wasn't being treated like a valuable asset to the Corps anymore, with the respect due his long and dedicated service. He was a danger now…even as he lie in a coma for the last three months.

Colonel Jack Diamond entered the cell-slash-hospital room ten minutes after the orderly left. He carried a small datapad in his hand and a grim look on his face.

"Another first, I see," the officer said without preamble.

Zac lifted his arms as far as the restraints would allow. "Isn't this rather extreme, colonel? It's been three months."

"Our precautions have proved necessary, sergeant. You just woke up without any chemical assistance. Imagine if you weren't restrained and could just waltz out of here as you please."

Zac was about to give up on military protocol, dispensing with the whole sir-yes sir thing.

"So what happens now?" Zac asked pointedly. "To tell the truth, that was an incredibly stupid thing to do, to jack me up to one hundred twenty percent. We're just lucky no one got seriously hurt—except me!"

Col. Diamond blinked several times, taken aback by the comment. "What do you mean, not seriously hurt?"

"Yeah, the guards. I remember seeing them moving as I ran into the passageway. And don't forget, I'm the one who got shot."

"C'mon, gunny," said Diamond. "You're telling me that that Rev-enhanced memory of yours is failing you now."

"No, sir, I can remember everything. I even remember how I *felt*. Isn't that what you were worried I'd do?"

"How convenient, Murphy." Zac noticed the ice-cold tone of the officer's voice. The man was seething with anger.

"Sir, did I do something to you in another life to make you hate me? You've had an attitude about me since we first met."

"No, sergeant, you didn't wrong me in *another* life. You're doing quite nicely doing it in this one. What about Manny?"

Manny Hernandez was the colonel's nephew. He was also Zac's closest friend, besides Olivia. "What about him?"

Diamond smiled. "And here I thought REVs could remember everything up to the time they were Twilighted."

"I wasn't Twilighted, sir; I was tranq'd."

"You say you don't remember?"

"I remember seeing him in the waiting room and then calling out to him. After that I blacked out."

"How convenient. Then maybe that explains *this*." Diamond worked his datapad and a video monitor flashed to life on the wall across the room from Zac's bed.

On the screen was a high-angled video of the waiting room, with Zac on his knees and covered in blood in the middle of a smashed glass coffee table. Manny was standing a few feet away, having just stood up from a couch. He had told Zac he would be waiting to see how the tests went....

There was an audio track in the video, and Zac heard his strained voice call out to his friend. Manny rushed forward, taking Zac by the hand. And that's when the scene turned into a nightmare.

Zac pressed off with his legs and tackled Manny, shoving him back onto the couch. Next, he wrapped his right arm around his friend's neck, spun around to his back, and literally twisted the man's neck in a circle. The break was so complete Manny's head was nearly ripped from his body.

Zac released the head, allowing it to flop forward, before falling back on the couch, his own body now just as lifeless as that of his dead friend.

Zac was beyond stunned; he felt sick. "Colonel...I, I."

"Belay that, Murphy. I've had three months to come to grips with your murder of my nephew, but seeing this now only makes me hate you more. Son, you are a danger, not only to the Corps, but to everyone you come in contact with."

"Sir, Manny was my friend! I wouldn't have done that if I wasn't jacked on Rev. I'm sorry, but I'm not responsible."

"Not responsible? You called him to you, and then twisted his neck into a pretzel—*before* you passed out. You knew exactly what you were doing."

"I don't remember."

"I don't care if you do or not."

Zac shifted his attention from the officer and the video screen several times. "I'm sorry."

Diamond turned off the video and firmed his square jaw, a purple vein in his neck bulging out. Zac could tell the career Marine was having a hard time dealing with the death of his nephew. Although he'd witnessed countless deaths in his career, Manny was blood. This was different. "I'm sorry too, son, but you're a menace. You asked what happens now? I'll tell you. You're being sent down."

"Sir, it was the drug, not me. Manny was my friend."

"*Was* being the operative word. And now we've been going round and round for the last three months trying to figure out what to do with you. I voted for direct termination, just an injection while you were in the coma, but the higher ups voted otherwise."

"I thought you said I was being sent down?"

Diamond laughed. "I meant you're being sent down to the surface of the planet we're orbiting."

"What planet?"

"Just some savage rock full of nasty beasts the surveyors call Eliza-3. You'll fit right in."

"Why there?"

"To put you on ice until a final verdict can be rendered. The scientist-types still think they can find a use for you. But seeing how you're unpredictable and out of control, I wouldn't count on that."

Zac lifted his shackles again. "Do I look out of control to you?"

"Not now, but it's obvious that can change at the drop of a hat."

"Sir…you guys made me what I am. I served a purpose in the Corps. I saved Marines' lives."

"And you will again, by not being the instrument of their deaths. We can't have such a lethal weapon such as you walking around making your own decisions. The Corps is about control and discipline, neither of which you can demonstrate with certainty. And given the chance, this would only be the beginning. Yes, Gunnery Sergeant Murphy, you *were* an asset to the Corps—when we could control you. Not so much anymore."

NOTES

Upon reviving from a drug-induced coma, there is a rare possibility the 0351-E may experience a heightened sense of hypertension and paranoia. This condition normally manifests within zero to ninety-six hours after waking. During this period, security personnel shall be assigned the 0351-E, not only for the safety of the individual but for those in close proximity.

- Command Directive, Joint Military Command, issued Sept. 4, 2082

9

A few minutes later, a whole cadre of guards and medical techs entered the room with a wheelchair. They released his restraints and dressed him in black and tan utilities and combat boots. Additional shackles were attached and he was set in the wheelchair. Then under heavy guard, he was wheeled from his room and down a series of narrow corridors as men with guns cleared the way.

Zac didn't recognize the ship; it was a different vessel and much smaller than the *Olympus*. Zac figured the huge star carrier had more important work to do than transport him to his waiting purgatory.

He was taken to the launch bay of the ship and wheeled to the rear loading ramp of a troop shuttle. Just as he entered the hatchway, he noticed Colonel Diamond behind the glass of the launch bay's control room. He smiled at Zac and gave him a salute. It wasn't the crisp and tight Marine salute, but one with the middle finger of his right hand extended.

Zac was wheeled into the shuttle and the wheelchair secured

to the deck. The door slid shut and minutes later he felt the loss of gravity as the vessel pulled away from the transport ship.

The troop compartment of the shuttle was devoid of windows, so Zac didn't have a chance to survey his new home from orbit. Instead, he suffered through the shifts in inertia and orientation until the craft dropped to a rough landing on the world known as Eliza-3. Guards unlocked his shackles from the wheelchair and pulled him up by the arms. Then they perp-walked him to the exit hatch with the leg and ankle shackles still attached.

And that's when he got the first glimpse of his planet-sized prison.

A blast of humid heat hit him as the hatch cracked and the ramp lowered. Through the doorway, Zac saw a thick jungle of broad-leafed trees and plants just beyond the blast radius of the shuttle. Moist grass had been charred by the landing jets, providing a narrow buffer zone from the jungle. With an entire planet on which to land, Zac wondered why the pilots had forced their way into the middle of a jungle. Surely there had to be wider LZ's somewhere.

Zac didn't have time to ponder the finer points of landing protocols before he was hustled out the shuttle and onto the spongy ground below. He stood wobbling, trying to regain his balance after three months in a hospital bed. Crewmen began unloading cargo crates, placing them at the edge of the jungle, and barely clear of the blast zone for take-off. At least they were leaving him something. He counted nine heavy plastic crates, and if given the opportunity, he would move them farther away from the LZ to keep them from being destroyed when the shuttle lifted.

Grim-faced guards unlocked his shackles while others stood several feet away, weapons ready. He rubbed his sore and swollen wrists while surveying the landing zone. He had been right about the pilots forcing their way in, but it wasn't as bad as it seemed. There was a wider area of thin foliage on the other side of the shuttle, providing a ringed clearing about a hundred feet in diameter.

Zac walked toward the stack of containers and began to move some of them into the jungle. He had no idea what was in them; he would take inventory as soon as the shuttle departed....which happened ten minutes later, with barely enough warning for him to bolt through the thick vegetation to put distance between him the burning heat and smoke of the lifting jets.

After the hot exhaust dissipated, Zac returned to the clearing, to find half of the remaining crates spread across the LZ, lids missing and contents strewn to hell and back. He recovered a canvas cot he found at the edge of the jungle, opened it and unfolded the legs. He sat down and scanned his new surroundings.

It had been deathly quiet only moments before. Now brave insects and other creatures were making their presence known, through a symphony of buzzing, clicks and whistles. The jungle was coming alive, and soon larger beasts would come to investigate the invader to their world.

With a deep sigh, Zac stood up, still shaky and uncertain from his long layup. He needed to get a camp formed and a fire going—even in the heat of jungle. Hopefully the flames would keep the creatures of the night at bay.

This was Day One of Zac Murphy's new life. He had to make sure he survived to Day Two, and every day from then on, until....

"So you're just going to leave him down there?" asked Arnie Patel, incredulously.

"That depends on you, doctor," Col. Diamond answered.

"Me?"

"That's right. On how your program turns out."

Arnie was confused. "My program? I thought all I was supposed to do is test the other 351-Cs? Are you saying that if I find more people like Zac that you'll do away with all this nonsense and take him off the planet?"

The Marine officer looked down at the smaller, pudgy man and frowned. "Nonsense? Do you even realize what we have here? You saw it with your own eyes. We had a fully charged REV who *didn't* activate. Hell, even his eyes didn't turn red."

"Not until you increased the dosage beyond any reasonable level, and with deadly consequences," Patel countered. The two men had argued this point ad nauseum for months.

"That's beside the point. When he did get the standard dosage, he looked just like the rest of us. Do you know what that means? It means he could walk down any city street and no one would have a clue how dangerous he is, not until he snapped. We had an activated REV who failed to activate."

"I would imagine you'd prefer that to the raving maniac you send out to kill everything he sees. This is an enhanced human being with superior abilities, and he's able to control the rage."

"That's exactly the problem, doctor," Diamond barked back. "*He* controls it, not us. When we activate a REV—a normal REV—we know exactly when he'll turn, and *we* control how long he remains activated. As long as we stay out of his way, everything is copacetic. With the damping influence of the naturally-occurring NT-4, we lose that control."

"So this is all about how best to use your magnificent weapon," Arnie stated.

"Of course it is!" Diamond growled. "I've been part of the oh-351 program for several years now, working with Cross and the others. I've seen all its incarnations, but we never imagined someone like Murphy coming from it. You're a doctor; can you explain how his body was able to spontaneously begin producing the drug on its own?"

"It's obviously a mutation of some sort," Patel answered. "He needs NT-4 to survive, and his body responded by giving it what it needs to *survive*—not to kill. He doesn't cascade out of control while on natural NT-4. That only happens with the synthetic, while you're in control, as you say. But now, with training and counseling, Zac may be able to return to normal society—"

The officer laughed. "Bullshit, Patel, this makes him even more dangerous. If it were up to me, Gunnery Sergeant Murphy would never leave that planet."

Arnie's frustration reached the breaking point. "You do realize he could be the first of a new breed of human, if his ability to produce natural NT-4 can be passed on to his offspring? Isn't that something worth our respect and care?"

Diamond's eyes opened wider, almost manic-looking. "Do you hear what you're saying? I, for one, don't welcome the idea of a bunch of crazed supermen with latent homicidal tendencies walking the face of the Earth. Give me a break, Patel."

"You make him out to be some kind of monster," Arnie snapped back. "If he is, then we created him."

"And that matters...why?"

Arnie let out a loud sigh. "So you're just going to leave him on that rock to die."

The Marine intelligence officer twisted the corners of his mouth into a smirk. "For the time being. If—or when—we learn how to control the beast, he could still be of use to us." Then Diamond glared at Patel. "And you better get to work finding out if there are others like him. We can't have any more ticking time bombs in the Fleet without us knowing about it. We need to know if we really have created a new breed of human, a stronger, more deadly type of man."

Patel met the angry eyes of the Marine officer. "I didn't think that was possible."

An hour later, Colonel Jack Diamond watched a screen in the ship's CIC as the image shifted from a high vantage point to another, skirting between the tops of huge, exotic-looking trees to get a better look. Murphy was sitting on a cot, looking defeated.

Diamond smiled. "Keep an eye on him, corporal," he commanded the enlisted man at the drone controls. "Report anything unusual."

"Unusual, sir?"

"You know what I mean…any superman-like stuff. We need to see how he adapts, overcomes and improvises. For him, it's a matter of life or death."

"Aye, sir. When will we be transferring to the surface?"

"The op site will be completed in a week. We'll go then—if he lasts that long."

"He's a Marine, sir; I pity the poor creatures that live on the planet."

"We'll see, corporal. Carry on."

NOTES

It's the lack of control that troubles me the most. The NT drug was supposed to enhance a subject's performance, not limit it to only a few simple basic emotions. At this point, I don't see much of a purpose for the drug, even in military operations. David disagrees. He's younger, with possibly more vision of what the program can become. I hope he's right. I'm becoming discouraged.

- Journal Entry, Nov. 9, 2071, Dr. Clifford Slater

10

Zac began collecting the supplies from the surrounding jungle and stacked them in the center of the charred landing zone. The ground here was mushy and wet, but it was the only open area he could see. He had nine plastic crates and began to fill them with the loose items. This allowed him to inventory his supplies even as he collected them.

Most of what he'd been left with consisted of small blocks of dehydrated food rations. He placed these in the containers and sealed the lids. He had no idea how long he'd be on the planet, so the rations would be saved as a last resort. He would live off the land for as long as he could.

There was a sleeping bag—just one—and four blankets. He had a solar heater, a water purifier, a hundred-foot length of rope and two solar-powered lamps.

But wrapped in one of the blankets he hit the jackpot.

It was a Marine survival kit, plus a few other items carefully packed so as to be hidden from his jailers. These included a twelve-inch long laser-edged hunting blade, along with a two-foot long machete. He also found a trusty black-bladed K-BAR knife.

He took the survival kit and sat it on the cot next to him. There was a note written in pencil on the canvas pouch.

I believe in you, the note began. *Stay with us. Love, Olivia.*

Even with his murder of Manny Hernandez, she still cared for him.

He unrolled the kit. Inside was a five-inch-long armband made of mesh and Velcro. On one of the faces was a variety of gauges, including a clock that could be adjusted to any time period, a compass, barometer, range-finder, thermometer, a small signaling mirror and a pencil-sized telescope. Also in a compartment along the length of the band was a first-aid kit made up of a scalpel, needles and sterile thread, plus antiseptic cream and two dollops of morphine. Just everything a boy lost in the woods would need.

Zac wrapped the band around his left forearm and secured it with Velcro strips. Surprisingly, he felt much better about his prospects looking at the tiny cache of loot he'd found. As a REV, he feared no man. Even in his passive state, he was three to four times stronger, with heightened senses and quicker reactions. And with the natural Rev in his system, he figured he was even more so. But the creatures on this world were an unknown. Even still, it wasn't fear he felt, but apprehension. Given time to assess a situation, he was sure he could survive just about anything this planet could throw at him...if he saw it coming.

He found the snap-up tent in the jungle and set it in the center of the clearing on a bed of huge palm fronds to keep it from sinking into the two-inch thick muck. With a pull of a cord, the one-man survival tent popped into existence. He unzipped the front and moved the cot inside, along with the sleeping bag. It was too hot to sleep in the bag, but it would help to cushion the utilitarian surface of the cot. He hooked one of the lamps to the overhead support pole. He was ready for the night, once he got a fire going.

He tucked the machete into his utility belt, and with the laser knife in his right hand, went out into the fringe of the jungle to gather wood. Surprisingly, the towering palm-like trees yielded an ample supply of dry wood, once the outer layer of fibrous bark was cut away. When dried, the bark would make excellent kindling.

He had trouble finding rocks on which to build his fire, but there were a few, mainly boulders weighing several hundred pounds which had failed to sink into the bog. With his REV strength he easily carried three of them to a place outside the tent, and then stacked the wood on top. The porous joining of the stones would provide ample draw for the fire. He used the laser edge of the knife, turned down in intensity, to start the fire. It flared up quickly. In the hot and humid jungle, the heat coming off the fire was nearly unbearable, but Zac could take it. His enhanced skin would insulate him against both hot and cold better than the average Human.

He scanned the horizon—what he could see of it from within the circular clearing of the landing zone. Far off in the distance were three peaks of a mountain range. The star for this system was beginning to touch the tallest of the peaks and would soon dip below, bringing Zac's first day on this planet to a close. He entered the tent and zipped it closed. The thick canvas material was designed to resist puncture, in case anything in the night decided to try to get to him. Even so, he kept the fire burning all night, getting up three times to add wood to the flames.

He slept very little, wakened often by the sloshy sounds of feet or paws in the wet mush outside. As it was with most jungles, it came alive at night, and curious creatures were studying him, taking in his scent, trying to determine where he fit on the food chain.

Beginning at first light, Zac Murphy would teach the inhabitants of Eliza-3 that there was a new Alpha male in town. They, like many of the species within the Grid, would soon come to learn that you don't mess with the Humans.

It was raining the next morning and his fire had gone out since the last time he added wood. But it was light outside and with his enhanced eyesight, he scanned the jungle looking for threats. Everything seemed calm, if not quiet. There were insects and other creatures, including a number of birds, all chirping and squawking for whatever reason.

Still dressed in his tan and black utilities and ankle-high boots, Zac stepped out onto the mushy ground and pulled a cube of rations from one of the sealed containers. Several of the boxes were moved or overturned, as beasts in the night tried to get inside. Now that he had locked the lids in place, they would remain secure, unless something carried one off into the jungle.

He walked to a large palm tree and guided a stream of water from one of the fronds into the opening in the cube. The package tore open as the food expanded. It was a bland tasting meat-like substance, but it did the trick. Also, the day before he'd found a sixty count bottle of vitamin supplements in the rations container. He popped one while contemplating the significance of the pill count. At one-a-day, his jailers didn't expect him to last more than a couple of months before having to live entirely off the land.

With his REV metabolism, Zac needed more calories than normal to maintain his lean body mass. With very little fat, he would begin to eat into his muscle very soon. He'd never experienced that before; he'd always been in the care of the Marine Corps and provided with everything he needed. He had about thirty days of standard rations, but that was for a normal Marine. He figured if he had to live off what was provided, he had about ten days of supplies.

He hiked into the forest, where he came upon several clusters of bamboo-like stalks. Using the laser blade, he cut one of the four-inch thick reeds. Sure enough, it was lightweight and segmented, but also incredibly strong. He cut a two-meter long stalk and sharpened one of the ends into a deadly needle point. With his speed and reactions, this should be enough to secure him a decent meal, if he could find something worth killing.

And with that, Zac Murphy went on his first hunting expedition for food—ever.

There was a lot of life in the jungle, including plenty of rabbit-like creatures with pot-bellies. They moved quicker than Earth rabbits, but Zac was able to spear a couple. With blood draining from the wounds and falling to the jungle floor, he began to make his way back to the camp.

That's when he heard the soft growl—or growls. In the mid-morning light, the jungle held areas of deep shadow, and in them he saw the yellow eyes staring out at him. The dead rabbits were stuck on the end of his bamboo spear, which he held in his left hand. He gripped the laser knife in his right.

Zac sensed the first attack coming from his right. He dropped the spear and spun to face his assailant. The beast sprung into the air, falling toward him. In an instant, Zac sized up the creature.

It was a huge, four-legged beast with a block head like a large pit bull. The mouth was wide and the muscles of the jaw pulled tight and bulged from the thick neck. But what made the animal most terrifying was the set of nine-inch long horns that protruded from its bony forehead. As it dove toward Zac, the mouth remained closed, relying on the horns to make the kill.

Zac swung the laser knife in front of him, slicing through the stubby snout of the huge dog and cutting the horns in half. A sharp, ear-piercing cry filled the jungle for only a second before the creature fell to the ground, a portion of its brains seeping from the wound.

The jungle came alive at that point, with the barking and yelping of a dozen other animals. Zac felt hot breath on his shoulder and ducked just in time as another of the deadly hounds came at him from behind. He fell to the soggy floor of the jungle and dropped the laser knife. The animal landed a few feet away, turned and charged again.

With his quickened reactions, Zac locked his fists around the two horns and twisted the beast onto its back, with him on top. Yellow, beady eyes stared at him from only inches away. Now the mouth opened, revealing inch-long teeth ending in needle points.

Zac had no problem controlling the huge beast by pressing and twisting the horns, but then a paw lashed out and ripped open the front of his utilities. The sharp claws cut into his flesh, but not too deep. He bled, yet felt little pain.

Another loud growl came from behind. He rolled, still gripping the horns of the beast but now pointing them upwards. A heavy weight fell on top of him and the first dog, followed by another loud squeal, as the third attacker became impelled on the horns of his pack mate.

Zac swung the head of the first dog, casting off his latest victim. Then he wrapped his strong legs around the torso of the first dog and twisted the horns until he heard—and felt—its neck snap. The beast stopped struggling.

Zac shoved both dogs away and stood up, scanning the shadows for more sets of yellow eyes. They were there, along with a cacophony of barking and yipping.

So Zac barked back.

The jungle leaves came alive as the surviving members of the pack scurried away, in fear of this new beast that had just killed three of their brethren.

Zac located his fallen laser knife and tucked it into the sheath on his belt. He looked at the three dead animals forming a circle of death around him. It reminded him a much smaller version of a Run. The two small rabbit-like things on his spear now looked inconsequential compared to the mass of the fallen dogs. But he also knew carnivores like the dogs would probably be tough and gamey; however, their hides could come in handy, either for clothing or leather strapping.

He picked up the bamboo spear and ran it through the neck of one of the dead dogs. Then he placed it on his left shoulder before grasping the loose fur of another dog, leaving the third to the jungle. Even with his superior strength, it was a load. Zac was panting by the time he made it back to the camp.

Zac was born and raised in Palo Alto, California, the son of engineers who worked long hours and made good money. They were indoor people, who seldom took vacations or communed with nature. As a result, Zac had never gone hunting as a child. Even his basic Marine training was light on survival techniques and completely devoid on how to field dress a kill. Although Zac had killed tens of thousands of aliens in his career, none had been for food. So it seemed odd that this supreme killer now stood over the set of dead animals without a clue what to do next.

He needed food—meat—so that seemed simple enough. Just scrape off the fur and cut off a chunk of flesh then lay it over the fire until done. But he also wanted the hide. How do you skin an animal? If you've never done it before, the task could prove daunting.

He made a mess of the first horn-dog, ending up with a sickening mass of organs and blood. But he did get a fairly decent-size section of contiguous hide off the animal. He also had a pile of lean meat ready to be cooked. Taking a strip of bamboo from his spear, he stabbed a slice of meat and dangled it over the new fire he'd started.

The second horn-dog proved easier to gut and skin. He figured in a week or so he'd be an expert, he wasn't too worried if his technique wasn't spot-on. Then he set into the rabbit-like animals. They proved easier to work with. Both were pregnant, which accounted for their pot-bellies. He wasn't sure if he should eat the fetuses, so he set them in the pile of innards which he then moved to the edge of the clearing. Even before he returned to the fire, jungle creatures were fighting over the scraps.

He was right about the horn-dogs; they were tough and gamey-tasting. The rabbits on the other hand, were delicious, not tasting like chicken, but beef instead. He looked at the bloody pile of dog meat. Considering the number of rabbits scurrying about the jungle, he didn't see any need to compromise. He carried the dog meat to the jungle edge. Moments later it sounded like an orgy of gastronomical delight, as dozens of creatures swept in for their piece of the pie.

Zac sat in the light rain on a cut log, letting the shower clean the blood from his uniform. It was mid-morning, and already he'd killed five animals, skinned them, and cooked his first meal on the planet. Now soaked to his skin, constructing a shelter beyond that of his small pop-up tent became the priority.

He returned to the crop of bamboo stalks, and using his laser blade, cut a dozen twelve-foot long lengths. Then using the rope, he looped them together and dragged the load back to the camp. He repeated this three more times until he had a decent stack of the four-inch-thick stalks.

Zac cut several into eight-foot lengths and laid them out on the ground. He then sharpened the tip of one of the twelve-foot lengths and placed it the middle of two sections of eight-foot long reeds, four feet wide. Using strips from the large palm fronds, he tied the pieces together. Next, he stood up the rickety structure and jammed the longer center piece into the moist soil, before creating a ninety-degree angle with the two sides. He retrieved the cot from the tent, stood on it, and used a rock to pound the twelve foot pole into the ground until the eight-foot tall side sections contacted the surface.

Next he fashioned a section of eight-foot long stalks together, but this one eight feet wide and with a pair of twelve-foot poles anchoring each side. He pounded the longer pieces into the ground and tied this new section to the narrower corner piece.

After a second ninety-degree section with a center anchor completed this part of his shelter. He stood back and admired his work. He now had a sixteen-foot-wide wall with two four-foot wide side sections set at ninety-degree angles, set firmly in the mushy bog.

He went out to cut more bamboo.

He didn't finish the shelter before dark, but as night fell he set the fire to blazing and munched down another helping of alien rabbit. He drank water dripping from the large fronds, captured in sections of the bamboo left over from the shelter. He returned to the tent for the night, and as he fell into an exhausted—yet satisfied—sleep, he felt he'd made progress. Conquering this new world might not be that difficult after all.

The next morning Zac finished the side walls to his shelter and cut a door in one face. He attached longer poles to support a couple of cross beams along the center line then set to work on the roof. He constructed a sixteen-foot wide section of twelve foot stalks and secured it with strips of animal hide to a cross pole along the top of one of the walls. Then using a twenty-foot-long bamboo pole—along with much of his REV strength—he lifted the panel up until if fell over and landed neatly on the high center beam of the shelter. He repeated the process on the other side to complete the pitched roof.

He built a ladder out of bamboo and then set about placing large palm fronds across the roof and sides of the hut. He closed out the exterior construction by placing a pair of triangular bamboo sections at each end of the a-frame openings in the roof.

He was just about to move inside to begin work on the floor, when he noticed two of the horn-dogs emerge from the thick vegetation of the jungle about fifty feet away. Zac took up his six-foot long bamboo spear, scanned the surrounding foliage, and waited to see if there was going to be a problem.

The dogs stood four feet tall at the shoulders and were formidable beasts. But this time they came to him with a rabbit stuck to the horns of one and another dead animal Zac didn't recognize on the other. They appeared docile as they approached to within twenty feet, and then to Zac's amazement, they lowered their front legs and bowed down, as if presenting him with their catch.

Zac came up to the animals, confident in his ability to defend himself, yet feeling he wouldn't have to. He took one of the impelled animals and used his laser blade to cut off a generous hindquarter. He laid it in front of the dog. He did the same to the other one. The beasts snatched up the fresh-cut meat and scurried off into the jungle.

Zac picked up the offerings and returned to his hut.

"Well, ain't that some shit?" he said aloud.

These animals—like all primitive beasts—relied on scent and pheromones to size up an opponent. The combination of his alien scent, along with the natural NT-4 coursing through his system, was telling a story to the creatures of the jungle. The horn-dogs were the largest and deadliest beasts he'd seen so far, and they were now bowing down to *him* and bringing food to their new master.

As Zac went to work building a base for the floor to his shelter, while thinking this wasn't such a bad gig if you could get it. *Leader of the Pack* had a nice ring to it.

NOTES

The Aliens Have Arrived! Finally.

- Headline, Los Angeles Times, Jan. 2, 2068

11

A week into his stay on the prison world of Eliza-3, Zac he'd already built a decent-sized shelter, complete with a ten-by-ten-foot deck outside the door. He cut a round hole in the middle of it and placed a bed of rock for his fire. He even had time to build a crude lounge chair out of bamboo reeds and cover it in palm fronds and the fiber of the tree bark.

He began to learn more about his environment, noticing how it seemed less hot and humid as he became acclimated to the weather. He also noticed something remarkable about the bamboo beds.

After cutting several down to the quick, he would come back a couple of days later to find they'd grown back by two feet or more. Although there were plenty of other bamboo beds around for his needs, he was amazed at how fast they grew back.

He also noticed a frenzied increase in animal activity in the jungle. In fact, when Zac would venture out, he would often have several of the rabbit creatures run into his legs as they scurried about in a mad rush. If the damn things weren't eating, they were humping. It was something to watch.

Another week went by before Zac—the ultimate REV warrior—became bored with sitting around on his deck, waiting for horn-dogs to bring him food, and with nothing else to do. So he packed some supplies in an animal-hide bag and set off for the mountains, which the range finder on his wrist band set at about thirty-five miles away.

There was a river about a mile from his camp which he had to ford. He delighted in the cool water, even as he watched for this planet's version of alligators and piranha. Finding none, he moved on to the distant foothills.

He reached his destination by dusk and spotted a set of caves set in the rock at ground level. There were others higher up, and one looked particularly interesting because of the stair-step arrangement of ledges needed to reach it. He climbed up and entered the cave.

It was fairly decent size, with a powdery floor of accumulated dust covered in paw prints. Fortunately, no one was home, so Zac cut wood from the forest below and started a fire near the entrance. The smoke rose up and vented out through cracks in the ceiling, using the open entrance to help with the draw. He slept in the sleeping bag that night, since it was cooler inside the cave than outside in the jungle heat.

The next morning he surveyed more of his surroundings. The cave would make an excellent backup shelter if it came to that. By then, however, Zac was enjoying his jungle camp. In his idle time, he'd built a wall around the compound by hammering bamboo stakes into the ground in a zig-zag fashion and then placing longer stalks horizontally between them. He tied the vertical members together to lock in the rest of the wall, surprised at how strong and sturdy the barrier became. It took him three days to complete the job, but once done, he felt strangely attached to the clearing in the jungle. Zac had never had a home before, not since leaving his parent's house at nineteen to join the Marines. After that it had been nothing but barracks and compartments aboard starships.

He left the cave and returned to his camp, finding only one of the horn-dogs waiting for him by the open entrance to the compound.

Growing up, Zac's family had owned two dogs, at separate times. One came to their home already named Nikko, and when he died, Zac insisted on naming the replacement puppy Nikko as well.

Now Zac bent down and scratched the head of the huge and deadly beast before pulling the carcass from its horns.

"From now on, you will be known as Nikko," Zac said with reverence. "Nikko the Third."

The tail of the dog began to wag, instinctively knowing from the tone of Zac's voice that a bond had developed between the two predators. Zac cut off a more-than-generous portion of the dead rabbit. Nikko took it up in his mouth, moved a few steps away, before beginning to eat it. This was a first. Usually he would run off into the jungle to feed.

Zac started a fire, cooked the rabbit and laid back in the lounge chair, staring up into the sky. The planet had no moon, so the nights were dark and the stars brilliant. As he was wont to do recently, he began to reflect on his life….

After joining the Marines at nineteen, Zac had gone through boot camp without a hitch. In fact, he reveled in the physical exertion and mental challenges he was put through. He had played sports in school but never excelled at anything. But now he was competing against other Marines and finding he was better than most.

The war with the Antaere had been going on for nearly a decade, with star travel a relatively new twenty-year-old event. And it wasn't the Humans who invented it.

The aliens arrived on Earth carrying a peace sign and wishing only to share a small portion of the planet while informing the awe-struck Humans about their rightful place in the Universal Order of things. It was something out of a science fiction movie, with half the population scared shitless, and the other half welcoming them to the point of worship. They were so Human-like, standing about six feet tall on the average, with similar faces and body structure. About the only thing that set them apart from us was the pale yellow of their skin. It was soon learned that their homeworld of Antara was remarkably Earth-like, and when they developed the singularity-gravity drive that resulted in faster-than-light travel, they discovered dozens of livable worlds, yet very few that matched their homeworld almost perfectly.

Zac grinned every time he thought how the Antaere got their nickname of *Qwin*. It came from the sound they made when scared or hurt. Zac hoped he'd done more than his fair share to keep the slang term alive.

After a few years on the planet, the Antaere began to get resistance to their spreading of the gospel on a planet that refused to accept the aliens as gods from the stars. By then, humanity was more pragmatic and secular, so they saw the Antaere as just another species from another planet and nothing special. But the aliens wanted more. They wanted a slavishly obedient race that would do their bidding.

Opposing expectations soon led to a conflict between the Antaere and their seemingly primitive subjects.

That was their first mistake.

The battle for Earth lasted three years before the Qwin were driven off the planet.

That's when their second—and much more serious—mistake became apparent.

In the seven years they had been on the planet, the Qwin had played fast and loose with their superior technology, bragging about it rather than protecting their secrets. By the time they were driven from Earth, the Humans had copied their gravity drive technology and followed the Qwin out into the Grid to seek vengeance, as well as territory for their own little stellar empire.

The politics was a confusing game, at least to those outside the centers of power. It had been the same throughout history. But now Gunnery Sergeant Zac Murphy was out of the fray. As he lay on his lounge chair, looking up at the distant stars, he thought how strange it was that he would find a type of peace on this planet, lost in the vastness of space. Before now, his life had been a long series of Runs and recovery, interspersed with a few brief periods of lull, with no time to think of an uncertain future. His future was Rev, as it was for everyone in the Program.

While in boot camp—and at his most vulnerable—Zac had been mesmerized by the heroic tales of the REVs. Feeling invincible at the time—as was the purpose of recruit training—he volunteered for the Program the day after graduating basic. Surprisingly, he passed the first stage of screening with little difficulty, especially in light of the huge numbers who didn't. Once inside, however, the reality of the process became stark and terrifying. In those days, almost half the applicants died from either the screening regimen or when they moved to the NT-4 trials. The war with the aliens was in full swing and the military needed all the weapons they could get, even the more exotic, such as REVs. The Human race realized the seriousness of the challenge they faced and gave the military a pass regarding their methods. Humanity needed a win, and at any cost.

The concept for the REVs had grown out of a need for a super weapon that didn't cost a lot to produce. In the past, the military had gone through both the robotic and mechanized phases, before discarding both as the answer to their operational goals. Robots proved too unreliable and costly. They could be easily hacked and cost a fortune to include all the artificial intelligence needed to make them an effective independent fighting force. Mechanized warriors—encased in eco-skeletons that enhanced their performance—were also costly and unreliable, and required extensive training to be operated at their theoretical potential, which was never fully realized.

When REV was first tested on Humans a couple of direct benefits immediately stood out. First, a single REV could do the work of a hundred robots or mechanized soldiers, and they didn't need expensive and elaborate programming to do so. And second, they were cheap and plentiful. In fact, it was impossible to keep the basic structure of a REV—in the form of people—from reproducing naturally and stocking the pool with countless new volunteers, no matter the inherent risks. It seemed like the perfect solution; cheap, renewable fodder for the ever-expanding war.

And the training was inexpensive, as well. Once a candidate made it into the Program, all that was required was to drill into the REV the need to kill anything that moved. It was truly *basic* training of the purest form.

And it worked.

Or at least it had until one of the REVs began to think for himself.

It was going on four months since Zac had a combat dose of NT-4, with nearly all the residual gone from his system. By all rights he should be dead. Yet here he was, very much alive and sustained by the natural NT-4 his body was producing. This fact opened up a whole new set of possibilities for Zac. If—and it was a big if—he was ever taken off the planet and forgiven for his murder of Manny Hernandez, the Marines would never risk jacking him up with a full dose of NT-4 again. This would change his status in the Corps, and make him eligible for retirement, possibly even with a medical disability. Seeing how he was getting by without the synthetic Rev, he was sure he could blend back into society and live out the remainder of his life as a normal human being. That was something he'd never seriously considered, until now.

Or they could just leave him on Eliza-3 to rot.

Zac's future lie somewhere between these two extremes.

NOTES

This new formula, designated NT-4, is showing great promise, not for sustained activation, but for brief periods. When used in conjunction with David's 'Twilight' drug, we've been able to sustain maximum levels for up to five minutes and save the subject from premature termination. Time to celebrate!

- Journal Entry, March 1, 2072, Dr. Clifford Slater

12

The next two weeks passed with excruciating monotony. Before being dropped on the planet, Zac had a purpose in the Marine Corps and was continually moving from one mission to another. Now he had nothing to do. Even his food was brought to him each day by his loyal horn-dog Nikko. Yet as a result of this need to keep busy he became a master at creating things out of bamboo and palm fronds, including a table and two chairs. He had no idea who would sit in the second chair, but making it kept his mind occupied.

He built a small second shelter to store his remaining rations. He also cut back on the vitamin pills to one every three days after discovering a variety of leafy plants along the shores of the river that didn't make him sick and provided more fiber for his diet. He found fruit in the jungle and a type of coconut milk in pods from the nearby trees.

Zac had conquered this new environment with aplomb. Now his greatest challenge became the mind-numbing boredom.

He awoke one morning feeling a distinct chill in the air; it was a welcome relief from the heat and humidity of only a few days before. Stepping out of the shelter and onto his bamboo deck, he noticed a coating of white on the three mountain peaks in the distance. Checking the barometer on his wristband, he noticed a drop in pressure. A storm was coming, and one that promised cooler temperatures.

He was prepared. He had already cut the two horn-dog hides into long coats. They did the trick, for as long as he wore them in the heat of the jungle. He had also fashioned a set of long galoshes from the skin to cover his military boots. They came to mid-thigh and were secured to his utility belt by straps of leather. He used them now and then when the mud in the compound got too deep after a heavy rain, or when fording the river on his many explorations.

He felt he was ready for whatever the change in weather would bring.

Near the end of daylight, Nikko lumbered into the camp, a food offering stuck on his horns. Zac went up to him and scratched behind his ears, even jostling him to wrestle. His daily interactions with another living creature were cathartic, but Nikko didn't want to play.

Disappointed—and a little worried for his loyal pet—Zac removed the dead rabbit and cut off the requisite piece for Nikko. The dog took the meat in his mouth, turned slowly and began to leave the compound. A few feet outside, he turned his huge head back to look at him. Narrow yellow eyes conveyed to Zac a look of sadness. Then the huge animal turned away and disappeared into the foliage.

Is he sick? Zac hoped not. Nikko was the only friend he had on the entire planet.

Zac feasted that night on Nikko's catch and then climbed into the sleeping bag for only the second time since arriving on the planet. It was noticeably cooler and he found the temperature conducive to a good night's sleep.

The next morning he awoke shivering and stiff. He dressed in the tattered remains of the utilities, slipped on his boots and draped an animal-hide coat over his shoulders. He was expecting cooler temperatures, but this was ridiculous.

Something was blocking the door from opening, but with a little effort he managed to push it away. It was snow.

Zac gasped as he surveyed the changed landscape outside. There was a layer of snow an inch or two thick on the deck and the floor of the compound. But that wasn't the most jarring transformation. It was the jungle.

Overnight, the once lush green foliage had changed to a uniform dark grey. The tall palms were now wrapped in their wide fronds, hugging the trunks for warmth. As he watched, he saw scrolls made of the smaller fronds being taken in under the large leaves to protect them from the cold. It was the most amazing thing Zac had ever seen.

With the jungle now nothing but a series of tall stalks pointing into the overcast sky, Zac could clearly make out the peaks of the distant mountains. They were covered in a solid layer of white, indicating to him that this was more than just a passing storm. Overnight the season had changed. It was now the dead of winter.

Or was it? This was probably just the beginning. It was bound to get a lot worse before it got better.

The next thing Zac noticed was the relative quiet of the converted jungle, relative because there was still sound everywhere. But unlike the scurrying of woodland creatures, there was only cracking and scraping as every plant, bush, tree and shrub was in the process of gathering up their leaves and branches to form a tight wrap around their vulnerable trunks. The sudden change in climate was part of the planet's routine, and everything that lived here—with the exception of Zac Murphy—was in the process of transitioning to the next stage.

Food!

The word hit him like a ton of bricks. He took up his six-foot-long bamboo spear and set out through the thin layer of snow into the jungle, which was more aptly a forest now. As he suspected, there was not a creature in sight. Zac was reminded of the strange behavior Nikko had exhibited the day before. The animal knew what was coming, and was either saying goodbye to the strange alien—expecting him not to survive—or was preparing to hunker down until the thaw came in the Spring. This also explained the frenetic mating ritual of the rabbits. There was only so much time to do what had to be done before the snows came.

Yet the animals had to go somewhere; they didn't all die off overnight. Zac reasoned that unlike the few animals of Earth that hibernated during the winter, this could be a planet were *everything* hibernated. This was not good. It meant things would indeed get worse, and without the resources to support even a few hardy breeds of plant or animal he could use for food.

He returned to the compound in a panic. Snow had begun to fall, lightly at first, but the imposing clouds overhead told him more was to come.

He went to the shelter covering his crates of supplies and ripped off the bamboo roof. He stacked the crates on top of the panel, taking a couple of the empty containers and packing them with other items such as his cot, sleeping bag and pop-up tent. He had to get to the cave along the foothills as soon as possible, a journey of thirty-five miles and in falling snow. He tied the crates to the bamboo sled and then wrapped the rope around his shoulders. If ever he needed the strength and endurance of a REV it would be today.

He set off for the mountains, towing the sled behind.

As he trudged through the ever-deepening snow, Zac could feel his body cascading, at least to a degree. As he had noticed before, this was a new experience for him. All the times he'd been activated as a REV he had no memory of the event. After a Run, he retained a photographic record of what happened, but it was like a silent video, with images only. He never felt his body or the sensation of becoming an operational REV.

Now he sensed the increase in strength and energy, along with a brightening of the scene as his eyesight grew more sensitive and his hearing more acute. Even his sense of smell seemed heightened. All in all, the natural NT-4 in his body was helping him survive and to press forward toward the distant mountainside.

By the time he reached the cliff face it was dark and he had a solar-powered lamp out leading his way, assisted by the compass on his armband. With the thinning of the forest trees, he spotted the dark circle that was the entrance to the cave a few miles before reaching the base of the cliff. The entrances to the other two caves at ground level were covered with snow, but not the one about a hundred feet above. Yet the stair-step ledges were.

He unhooked the sled and made his way up to the cave, clearing the steps as he went. The chamber was empty; he was expecting some hibernating animal to have claimed it for his own. That would have been fine by him. At least he'd have something to eat this evening rather than his rapidly dwindling rations.

He shuttled the crates up to the cave before breaking out the cot, sleeping bag and all the animal-hide coats and other blankets he had. The small heater he'd been supplied with—and which he hadn't used since his arrival—was now set on full and placed next to the cot. He was exhausted, cold and hungry. He melted some snow with the heater and hydrated a block of rations. It satisfied his hunger for the moment, if not his loss of precious calories after the long hike.

He crawled under the load of coverings and in a few minutes was sound asleep.

The next morning he checked the charge on the heater. It would need a couple of hours of bright sunlight to recharge, but the gloom from outside the cave told him it could take all day, if even then. Fortunately, the entrance was kept clear of all but blowing snow by a prominent overhang. He stepped outside and surveyed the winter wonderland laid out before him…except he didn't see it as much of a wonderland.

What he saw were miles upon miles of thick snow cover. The cold had frozen all except the top layer that was still accumulating from a light, but steady snowfall. He was in desperate need of heat, so he dressed as warmly as he could and took his machete and laser blade down to the forest floor. The laser function of the knife had stopped working a couple of weeks before; the delicate circuitry was notorious for breaking down in the field. But he could still use the sharp metal edge. However, the machete would be his main wood-gathering tool.

He set to work on the nearest tree—a former palm—now a grey pole wrapped in an equally grey shroud of fronds. To his surprise, when he cut through the fronds, he found the fibrous bark underneath to be dry and healthy. He sliced off a good portion of it and put it in an animal-hide bag. He would use it for kindling, just as he had when the forest was a jungle.

Then he cut into the tree itself. Again, the wood was dry and laced with seams of maple-scented pitch. He whacked at the tree for several minutes, chipping off decent-size chunks for his fire. He bundled up the cuttings with rope and hauled them to the cave. He spent most of the day collecting wood, again driving himself to the point of exhaustion.

His labors proved successful. By nightfall he had a tall pile of wood and kindling, with a roaring fire blazing at the entrance to the cave and a smaller one near the cot, which he had positioned along the inner wall of a small alcove. The heat radiated off the rock, turning the interior of the cave maple-scented and toasty. He smiled as he peeled off the shirt of his utilities to let the warmth soak into his skin.

His mood took a turn for the worse when he looked at the two plastic crates containing his remaining rations. One was full, the other half-empty. Without another source of food, he figured he had about six days left, and that was just at subsistence level. His REV body needed more than average caloric intake.

Zac spent a restless night in the warm cave agonizing over the challenge he faced. If it wasn't one thing, it was another….

NOTES

"It's a dynamo effect, where energy is fed into a finite space until it collapses into a microscopic singularity—a black hole," explained Dr. Larry Nash. "The Antaere gravity generators are able to do this on a continual basis, creating event horizons which their spacecraft hover just inside of. It's an absolutely incredible process that we're only now beginning to understand."

- Except from an article, Washington Post, dated Feb. 4, 2069

13

The next morning dawned cold but clear. Before heading out in search of food, he cut sections out of a lid to one of the empty crates and formed a pair of crude snow shoes. He used leather straps to secure them to his fur galoshes. As he set out with his trusty bamboo spear, machete and K-BAR knife, he struggled keeping the shoes on his feet. After half a dozen starts and stops he finally settled on a decent compromised. It wasn't pretty, and it was awkward, but at least they kept him from sinking into the snow.

He was an hour into his hunt—with absolutely no luck—when he came upon a flurry of paw prints in the soft top layer of the freshly fallen snow. His heart leapt. Here were animals still awake and roaming the forest. There had to be food for them—and in a worst case scenario—they would be food for him.

He studied the prints. They had wide pads with deep indentations on one side indicating long, sharp claws. Zac figured they were a form of native wolf. He set off following the direction of the tracks.

A few minutes later he stopped suddenly, sensing that something wasn't right. He turned slowly to see the first of the animals slowly creeping up behind him. It was indeed wolf-like but a little smaller. It had silver-gray fur and what appeared to be a boney ridge plate running down the spine to its powerful hunches. The snout was long, with moist black nostrils that flared in the cold air. Frosty clouds of breath escaped from the mouth as it snarled at him, revealing top and bottom rows of needle-sharp teeth. Pale gray eyes stared unblinking at him as the beast continued to approach.

He heard a low growl to this right and turned to see another of the native wolves appearing from behind a tree. A quick scan found a dozen more, staying back in the distance as the lead force closed in on him.

Zac was sure none of the wolves had seen a creature like him. His scent was strange and his danger unknown. They were being cautious until they knew the extent of the threat or the taste of his flesh.

As the main predator drew near, Zac used his enhanced REV reactions to snap out with the bamboo spear and slap the beast in the snout. Surprised, the wolf jumped back, yipping before lowering its head and giving out an even fiercer growl. Another of the approaching animals got within range, and Zac whacked it across the side of the head. There was confusion within the pack. They weren't used to food that fought back. A few more slaps and the pack gave up on this obstinate prey. They yelped and barked at they ran off into the woods.

Zac followed. He didn't want to kill the hunters, content to let them lead him to a steady supply of food. He also didn't want to chase them away too far if they were territorial. He needed their skills and familiarity with the local landscape.

Eventually he heard a loud series of yipping and howls. He stepped up on a low hill where he could look down on a small clearing between the gray trees. The wolves were going crazy, running around in circles and burying their long snouts into the snow before withdrawing them and howling some more. Then they began to dig, using long claws to cut through ice and snow. Most disappeared completely in the tunnels, before emerging a moment later with a bloody animal in their jaws.

Jackpot! Zac thought. The wolves' heightened sense of smell allowed them to locate hibernating animals under the snowpack, and now they were running around, covering the virgin snow in a gruesome spray of bright red blood from the bodies of their prey.

Zac entered the fray. The wolves growled at him and moved away. Desperate not to let them get away, he jumped on one of the wolves and pressed its huge head into the snow.

"Drop it!" he commanded, slapping the head with the end of his spear. The wolf didn't comprehend; all it knew was that someone was trying to take its food away. It growled and struggled, before finally dropping the animal and taking a snap at Zac. He shoved the wolf away and grabbed the bloody carcass.

The other wolves ignored him, while his disgruntled victim ran off to dig a second hole. A moment later he was rewarded with another catch, and forgot about his humiliation at the hands of this strange new predator.

Zac lashed out with his stick, slapping the skulls of two other wolves until they dropped their catch. He snatched them up before others of the pack could get to them.

Five minutes later it was over. The pack had harvested all the food they could from this field and ran off looking for better hunting grounds.

Zac was ecstatic. He had seven dead animals, most the tasty rabbit creatures his diet had consisted of for the past two months. His stomach growled at the prospect of a decent meal. He double-timed it back to the cave, as best he could in his flimsy snowshoes. With a full belly and ample heat, he would make a better pair. He would need them to track his new friends.

The one advantage found in the cold of winter over the heat of summer was that Zac was able to field dress several of the rabbits and place them in the ice outside the cave for future consumption. This allowed him to stockpile food, having to go out only once every four days or so to track down the wolf pack and abscond with part of their catch. The beasts learned quickly, and most surrendered their prizes with only a wave of his stick, rather than a whack to the head. There was plenty of food for everyone, even if some of the wolves had to do double duty to keep Zac happy.

As the days passed, and he learned more about how to survive in the winter of his prison planet, Zac discovered something about the trees he used for firewood. If he cut into a section, exposing the interior to the cold, the next day the tree would be limp and soggy and on the verge of death. The shield from the cold had to be maintained for the tree to survive. Once cut, it would die.

So he began to harvest whole trees at a time. It wasn't that there was a shortage of them, it just a seemed a waste otherwise. Soon a full third of the cave was stacked with firewood, with long strings of bark-kindling hanging from rock ledges.

And then the routine set in. Even though he had to go out only infrequently to gather food, he savored his time in the woods. The hide coats kept him warm and his new snowshoes worked great. He even took a length of bamboo from the sled and split it in two, forming a crude set of skis. He didn't use them for downhill treks, but rather cross-country. They did the job.

Three weeks into his stay in the cave, Zac was experiencing the same malaise as has he had at his jungle compound. He was bored senseless. And he didn't even have the universal utility of bamboo stalks to keep him occupied. All he did was whittle on some of the logs and wait for the next time he could get some exercise tracking down his friendly pack of wolves.

That all ended, however, when he heard the sonic boom.

At first he thought it was a thunder clap. They were common in the cold, thin air of the mountains. But this one sounded different. He rushed to the cave entrance to have a look.

Sure enough, using his REV-enhanced eyesight, he detected a shuttlecraft circling for a landing some distance away. He checked the rangefinder on this armband. Twenty miles out. He noted the heading on the compass and sighted along a set of gray trees the location of the shuttle as it dipped from view.

Zac shook his head. "How stupid do they think I am?" he asked aloud. He'd begun to say a lot of things out loud these days, a defense against the unnatural silence of his surroundings.

He recognized the type of shuttle. These vehicles were tasked with delivering Marines to a battlefield, and not announcing their arrival with a boom that could be heard for fifty miles in all directions. No, the sound was for his benefit, which revealed another truth he had long suspected.

He was being watched.

One did not set a prisoner on a planet without some form of monitoring. If not, then just kill him and get it over with. The Marines were keeping an eye on him; hell they might even have a mosquito drone in the cave, watching his every move. And now they were letting him know they were here.

And when the shuttle lifted off less than five minutes later, creating a second shock wave as it raced for space, he knew another REV like himself had just been deposited on the planet. The sneaky bastards had tried to make it not so obvious by placing the new prisoner twenty miles away. But Zac understood the meaning. What frustrated him the most was that the people in charge of this fiasco expected him to believe that the location was just a matter of chance.

Tomorrow Zac would head out and fetch the other REV. At least then he'd have another person to talk to, other than himself.

NOTES

Ten minutes! We've been able to take a subject up to ten minutes and bring him back down. This does tend to increase the residual effects of the drug on the system. Fortunately, the small amount of NT-4 remaining in the body mitigates the effects.

- Journal Entry, March 8, 2073, Dr. Clifford Slater

14

The next morning, Zac dressed in a horn-dog coat, fur galoshes, snowshoes and a rabbit skin hat. He placed the second coat and snowshoes in one of the empty crates, along with his sleeping bag, blankets, solar heater and lamp. He secured it to the bamboo sled and wrapped the load with rope. He was pretty sure the other REV would be ill-prepared for the Eliza-3 winter. He could help with that.

He set off in a light snowfall, towing the sled behind. He made good time over the twenty-mile hike. This was the farthest out he'd gone in a while; his wolf pack was territorial and stayed within ten miles or so of the cave. That was convenient. But now he enjoyed working his muscles harder. He wasn't cold and the load was light for a REV. He was actually humming to himself when he reached the camp of the second REV.

The man obviously hadn't had time to get his act together. The supply crates were scattered chaotically in deep snow drifts, left where they fell after being pushed out the back of the shuttle the day before. The REV did manage to find the tent, which was now erected on a solid sheet of ice, with the glow from both the solar heater and lamp illuminating the interior.

Zac stepped to within ten feet of the canvas shelter.

"You in the tent! It's Zac Murphy."

All the 351-Cs knew each other, if by name only.

A shadow moved inside, and the zipper came down half way. A bald head appeared, highlighted by brilliant blue eyes, tight lips and a frown.

"Murphy…there goes the bloody neighborhood." The man's eyes locked on Zac's. "I thought you were dead."

"Not hardly." Zac looked around at the mess that was the camp. "Listen, mister, I'm in charge of maintaining the grounds around here, and I certainly can't allow you to litter like this. I'm going to have to ask you to organize your camp better. Otherwise you'll have to leave."

"Bite me. I kinda like it here. And you couldn't kick me off this planet even if you tried."

The zipper came all the way down and the huge man stepped from the tent wearing a thick winter coat. Zac stepped up to him and they gave each other a heartfelt man-hug.

"Staff Sergeant Angus Price, fancy meeting you here."

"That's Gunnery Sergeant Price to you. I made E-7 about a year back." The man's thick cockney accent seemed more pronounced through the chattering of his teeth.

"Congratulations," Zac said. "I see your new stripe got you choice of duty station. Wait until you see the ski lodge. Hot totties and even hotter snow bunnies."

The smile vanished from Price's face. "Seriously, gunny, let's get back in the tent. It's fucking freezing out here."

They crowded into the tent and Angus zipped it close. The tiny heater was working overtime and barely making a dent in the freezing temperature. Clouds of breath filled the air.

Zac reached out a hand and ran it over the winter coat Price was wearing. "I didn't get one of these in my welcome kit; I had to make my own."

"You do realize that thing stinks to high heaven."

"You'll get used to it. I have one for you, too."

There was a cot in the tent. Angus pulled it to the center and the two men sat down, straddling it at both ends.

"Okay, Zac, what the hell is going on?"

"What did they tell you?"

"Nothing! All I know I was pulled off my ship and put through a lot of tests. Arnie Patel—he was your doctor, wasn't he—he did the tests. Then all of sudden I'm told I have new orders. I'm loaded on a ship and the next thing I know I'm being kicked out the back of a shuttle and up to my waist in snow. No explanation, no nothing, just a slew of nervous looking sailors pointing guns at me as they tossed a bunch of crates out the back. Hell, I barely had time to get away before being roasted by the lift-off jets."

Zac huddled near the heater, rubbing his hands together for warmth. He smiled. "Well my friend, have I got a story for you."

They spent the rest of the day with Zac relating the story of natural NT-4 and of events that led them both to become residents of beautiful and exotic Eliza-3. When he was done, Angus stared at him for a full thirty seconds, his jaw hanging slack. There were frown lines on his forehead.

"And this natural NT-4 will keep us alive?"

Zac knew his friend was concerned with the fear every REV lived with, that of their bodies burning up without the maintenance boosts.

"It's been over six months since I had a combat dose, and I'm still here."

"Yeah, but you're different from the rest of us."

"Not really. *You* wouldn't be here unless the same thing was happening to you. When was the last time you went on a Run or had a boost?"

"It's been over two months now, and that's what's worrying me."

"Relax buddy, I think your days of having to worry about getting your NT-4 fix are over."

Angus looked around the tent. "I hope you're right, 'cause we ain't be gettin' no Rev around here," he said using his best American slang. Then he turned serious. "So they're just going to leave us down here until they figure out what to do with us?"

"It's a test, Angus, a test to see if we can co-exist without killing each other."

"If that's the case, then I'll go first."

Zac snorted. "Getting cocky since you put on the extra stripe, aren't you?"

The smile vanished from the face of the huge Englishman. "And Manny…damn."

Zac shook his head. "I swear I don't have any recollection of what happened."

"But they have a video?"

Zac nodded. "You know we've never been held responsible for any psychotic breaks or for accidents during a Run. I think this is just more of the mind-games they're playing."

Angus had a small stack of rations resting on the floor of the tent. He picked up two and handed one to Zac. A small flask of melted snow activated the packets.

"So what now?"

"First we cuddle here for the night and then head back to the cave in the morning. It's a pretty sweet set-up, so we'll be fine."

"For how long?"

"That, Gunnery Sergeant Price, is the million-dollar question."

"I thought it was the six-four thousand dollar question?"

"That's in adjusted-dollars, my friend. You really do need to keep up with current events."

Angus was impressed with Zac's cave once they returned the next afternoon, towing an overloaded sled with a new supply of rations. They would be welcome, if unnecessary. It was always good to vary a diet, and a helping of even processed mash potatoes and gravy would hit the spot.

A few days later—after Angus became a little more acclimated to the weather—Zac took him hunting with the wolf pack. The skittish animals were weary of him at first, definitely apprehensive of the new alpha male and his strange smell. He stood back as Zac collected a double helping of hibernating rabbit before leading the nearly-frozen REV back to the cave.

"Three months…amazing. You've done quite well for yourself," he said as Zac expertly prepared the rabbits for the fire.

"All I did was improvise, adapt and overcome. Isn't that what we're supposed to do?"

"And the seasons changed almost overnight?"

Zac nodded. Then he turned serious.

"They let me know you were here with the sonic boom, which proves we're under surveillance. They wouldn't be watching us unless they have plans. Otherwise just let us rot."

"So it's just a matter of time," Angus said. He looked around the cave. "Shouldn't be a problem. So what do you do around here for entertainment?"

"I whittle a little."

"That's it? Do you play chess?"

"We don't have a chess set."

"We can whittle one."

Zac grimaced. "It's been years. Even then I wasn't very good."

Angus flashed a wide smile, his blues eyes alight in the flickering camp fire. "Then we'll play for money."

"We have no money either, unless you suggest we whittle that, too."

"I'll take a marker. I'm sure you're good for it."

When the second sonic boom came two weeks later—and much closer—Zac was relieved. He owed Angus twenty-four thousand a-dollars from his chess losses. Maybe this new arrival would give Angus a better game.

The shuttle dropped barely ten miles away; Zac hoped it didn't scare his wolf pack away. They were a REVs best friend during winter on Eliza-3.

Zac repeated the same story for the new arrival; another E-7, 351-*Charlie*, named Mike Brickey. He was a twelve-year veteran of the program, second in seniority to Zac. He had been put through the same routine as Angus, arriving confused and mad as a hornet.

"This is crazy! There are three of us now…and we're not tearing each other's throats out. How much longer are they going to keep us here?"

Zac smiled. Mike had only been on Eliza-3 for four days and already he was getting impatient.

The next morning, Zac went out on the ledge outside the cave and began to yell. The other two REVs joined him, first out of curiosity, and then with understanding. They screamed and made obscene gestures for about fifteen minutes until they got bored and their throats raw. Three hours later they were at it again.

For the next two weeks, when not hunting with the wolves or losing at chess to Angus, the REVs went through the same ritual. If anyone was watching they would get the message: *Enough is enough! Let's get on with it.*

The next time a shuttle landed, it came without sonic boom and set down in the clearing at the base of the mountainside below the cave. After the smoke cleared, a side hatch opened. Zac and the others took nothing with them, not even the animal-skin coats. They walked down the steps and into the waiting spacecraft.

Thirty seconds later they were up and away, heading for space.

NOTES

It was always my hope that NT-4 would allow for increased abilities without the horrible side effects. It doesn't look like this version of the drug will do it. In fact, we seem to be getting further away from that reality. I'm getting too old for this.

- Journal Entry, August 10, 2073, Dr. Clifford Slater

15

As Zac suspected, the shuttle—and the starship it docked with—were remotely piloted. No one was going to risk a crew with three REVs onboard, especially when they were producing their own version of NT-4.

The transport ship was a *Birmingham*-class frigate that normally carried a crew of twenty-five, so Zac, Angus and Mike had plenty of room to move around. They also found a fully-stocked galley, ample water for long, hot showers and lockers with clean uniforms in their sizes.

They showered, shaved and slept, and then on the third day out, a video screen flashed on in the small mess hall attached to the galley. All three men were there at the time, which told Zac they were being monitored.

The always smiling face of Colonel David Cross gazed down at the seated trio.

"Welcome, my friends," the Marine doctor said jovially, as if greeting co-workers over for an informal dinner. "I'm glad to see you are all well."

Seeing the Marine officer only infuriated Zac more. It was his experiments which resulted in Manny's death and left Zac stranded for three months on a savage world.

"Excuse me, but what was all that crap about?"

"You mean the planet?" Cross asked sincerely. Did he really not know what Zac was talking about? "It actually started out as people said, as a place to hold you until we figured out a use for your new newfound abilities."

"Abilities, and what are those exactly, sir?"

"That depends on who you talk to," Cross said. "For me, it was your ability to survive without NT-4."

"You knew that before you sent me down," Zac countered.

Cross shrugged. "It was a theory, now confirmed."

"And we're like that, too?" Angus asked. He still hadn't bought into the idea of not needing maintenance boosts.

"That's what the tests confirmed…as far as your ability to produce natural NT-4. We'll know more when you arrive at the camp."

"What camp?" Mike Brickey asked.

"Camp Slater, a research and training facility on Borin-Noc—you might know it as ES-6."

"Training facility?" Zac said. "Training for what?"

"To become a team, gunny, what else?" Cross was beaming with pride. "I spent quite some time trying to convince the higher ups about the unique opportunity we have to create the most powerful and effective special operations unit ever. Never before have REVs been able to work in conjunction with one another. Imagine what you can do as a team."

Zac shook his head. "We're not full REVs, colonel. You know that. We're just a handful of men with a different kind of Rev in our systems, and not anywhere near combat strength." Zac tensed. "I hope you're not thinking about activating me again. I don't think I'd like that very much."

Cross shook his head. "We're not advocating that at all, sergeant. We would prefer if you operated on just the natural NT-4. It really is quite remarkable, something we envisioned the synthetic to be many years ago. Unfortunately, artificial NT-4 never allowed for the level of control we now see with the organic version."

"I'm glad I could help," Zac said. "But aren't you forgetting what Colonel Diamond said, that we can't be allowed to think on our own? That would be too dangerous. What changed in three months?"

"Diamond—and the others—were speaking from a position of ignorance. We have had more time to consider the possibilities. I assure you attitudes have changed. Now we have a second chance to study this mutation more closely. Have patience, gentlemen. As with most things having to do with you, we are learning as we go."

"That's what you said the last time you jacked me up. What did you learn from that experience?"

"I understand you're bitter—"

"I killed one of my best friends…and then was accused of doing it on purpose!"

"I am working on getting the records expunged, gunny."

"Thanks for that. Be sure to put in a good word for me at my court martial."

"There will be no charges, Zac. I assure you."

"And why should I trust you—"

"How long until we get to Camp Slater?" Mike asked, stepping into the conversation in an attempt to defuse the flaring tempers.

Cross continued to glare at Zac for a moment, before shifting his attention to Mike. "You have another six days. So try to relax. There are videos and books in the computer. There's even a very challenging chess program for you, Sergeant Price."

Zac grew even more furious. *So they did have a camera in the cave. And still they kept me on that planet for three months...and for no good reason.*

"Is there anything else, *colonel?*" Zac barked, tiring of the officer's irritating voice.

Cross's expression changed. Gone was the goofy smile and giddiness, replaced now with a stern, square jaw and piercing gaze. Zac had never seen such a hard look from the lab geek before.

"*I* will tell you when the conversation is over, *Gunnery Sergeant Murphy.*" The voice was cold as ice. "You fail to understand that I'm on your side. You think I only see you—all of you—as just lab rats, good only for study. You're wrong. I see so much more, so much potential for what you *can* become. I only wish to understand the process better, for all our sakes. So a little fucking gratitude would be nice...sergeant!"

Zac was taken aback by the outburst. Here was another side to David Cross he didn't know existed.

"Forgive me, sir. I'm just tired and frustrated. I appreciate your help."

Cross didn't back down. "That's better," he growled. "*Now there is nothing more. I will see you on Borin. Until then, try not to fuck anything up.*"

The screen went black.

Mike and Angus were looking at him, stunned.

"That went well," Mike said. "Nothing like pissing off the inventor of Rev."

"Slater invented Rev," Zac corrected, timidly.

"Slater's dead. All we have left is Cross, so play nice. We might live longer if you do."

NOTES

Although their society is based on a devote belief in their religion of the Order, the leadership of the Antaere is centered on the Zaphin bloodline, which can trace its origins back over two thousand years, to a time even before the introduction of their religion.

- High school textbook, Austin Unified School District, 2069

16

All ES worlds were nearly exact twins of Earth in terms of size, gravity, length-of-day and more. They also had the usual variety of climes. Camp Slater was located in a desert.

Zac thought it appropriate. Over the last three months he'd experience tropical rainforest, harsh alpine winter and now desert. Why not? It keeps a person guessing.

The remotely-piloted frigate came to a dusty landing in a wide valley expanding out from the confluence of two barren mountain ranges to the north. The three REVs were on the bridge, looking out the main viewport during the landing. As they descended, they spotted a row of Quonset huts with a larger building placed between them to the north. Farther south was what looked to be a firing range, along with other compounds housing a variety of other structures. Dirt roads ran between the components of the camp. No other settlements could be seen nearby.

When the dust settled and the side hatch of the starship

opened, Zac and the others stepped out into the brilliant light of mid-day on this world. Surprisingly, it wasn't hot. This must be winter on this part of the planet. Still, it was a lot warmer than winter on Eliza-3. Zac pushed away his observations of the weather to concentrate on the two men who just climbed out of an open-air transport and were approaching the shuttle.

One was a Marine officer—a major—while the other was a muscle-bound black man towering well-over six-feet tall and wearing the chevron of a master sergeant. He had the look of one: stern and confident. Zac and the others were wearing uniforms and covers; they saluted the officer.

The man returned the salute and then reached out to shake each of their hands.

"Welcome to Camp Slater, gentlemen. We've been anxious for your arrival."

As the default leader of the REVs, Zac simply replied: "Thank you, sir." He would reserve further comment until he had more information.

"I'm Major Ryan Elliot. I will be your division commander while you're here." He motioned toward the angry-looking senior enlisted man. "This is Master Sergeant Darius Bullock." The officer smiled. "His friends call him *Bull*. He will be your lead instructor during the training phase."

The man made no greeting, nor did he offer to shake their hands. He continued to stare at the three REVs like he wanted to rip their heads off. Zac didn't take it personally. If he was indeed a drill instructor, this was all part of the persona.

The officer turned toward the row of buildings off in the distance.

"Let me give you a brief rundown as to the layout of the camp. The tall canvas building in the center is the hospital." Zac thought the large red cross above the door was a dead giveaway.

"The huts to either side are numbered one to eight, starting on the left. Number one is supply, followed by barracks in two through four. You will be in Hut Four, next to the hospital. There you will meet the other two members of your team."

"Other two?" Zac asked.

"Yes, Gunnery Sergeants Donovan Ross and Kyle Johnson."

Zac knew one personally, the other by name. "No shit...sir? I thought it was just the three of us."

"So far there are five. I'm told others may qualify in the future, but so far this seems to be it."

Zac thought the word *qualify* seemed strange. He wondered just how much the officer knew?

Major Elliot returned to his narration. "Hut Five on the right side of the hospital contains the mess hall, number six admin, and the other two are training facilities." He turned more to his right. "There's the firing range, along with a variety of tactical courses and assault buildings."

He turned back to the REVs. "You'll get more details later, but the general routine calls for you to begin each day with a visit to the hospital where baselines will be checked and recorded. After that you can have breakfast. The mess hall is open from oh-six-hundred to twenty-hundred. Your barracks hut was designed to hold twenty senior enlisted, so you'll each have your own rooms, with no regard to rank. They're all the same. And speaking of that...."

Major Elliot reached into his pocket and withdrew what looked like a small ring box. He handed it to Zac.

Inside was a single gold metal bar.

"What's this, sir?"

"It's your promotion to second lieutenant, Mister Murphy. Command figures they'll need someone to blame if things go wrong." The officer smiled, having no idea how sensitive the subject was. Angus and Mike looked at Zac, half expecting a blow-up. Instead, Zac remained calm, if resistant.

"Sir…I don't know."

"Relax, Lt. Murphy. If you think about it it's actually a pay cut. But it will require your team to salute you."

"We'll see about that," Mike said into his hand.

"Very good then," said Elliot. "I will now leave you in the capable hands of Master Sergeant Bullock. Sergeant…."

Major Elliot returned to the transport and was driven away, leaving the rest of them standing at the edge of the spaceport, about half a mile from the buildings. Bullock stepped closer.

"So you're REVs?" he said as sarcastically as possible. He eyed them up and down, with Angus being the only one even close to the man's size and height. "Let me tell you what's going to happen here," Bullock growled. "I'm responsible for turning you into Marines. I know you consider yourself to be Marines already, but you're wrong, dead wrong. Sure, you skated through basic about a century ago, but all that did was *prepare* you to become Marines. And then the three of you took the easy way out. You volunteered to become REVs. Since then all you've known how to do is one thing…run. Well real Marines don't run…we charge!"

He turned and pointed to the nearby firing range. "There you will learn how to fire real weapons, and not simply point your arm and pull a trigger. In the other compounds you'll learn assault tactics, squad maneuvers and sniper skills. In the gym you'll be taught hand-to-hand combat, both defensive and offensive. Until now, all you've done is kill in mass. It doesn't take a lot of skill to hit a target when there's a hundred Qwin standing in front of you. Now you'll be taught how to kill, selectively and with deadly efficiency."

He stepped up to Zac, looking down at him, noses only

inches apart. "And rank don't mean shit to me, *lieutenant*. If you screw up—any of you—you'll answer to me." He stepped away. "And believe me, I'm no pussy Qwin."

He spun on a heal to face the buildings. "Now double-time it to Hut Four."

Bullock took off at a fast trot. Zac and the others followed.

A few feet into the run, Mike sprinted ahead, reveling in the freedom of the open space and fresh air. Angus caught up to him and kept going. Zac accepted the challenge and ran ahead of both of them. Soon it was an all-out sprint between the three REVs, their bodies already stronger than a normal man's, but now experiencing a slight cascading effect, making them even stronger.

They reached the barracks—a distance of half a mile—forty seconds later. It would be a record on just about any world, if anyone was taking notice.

Master-Sergeant *Bull* Bullock stopped his quick jog and stood in awe of what he just saw. He turned to his right, toward the admin building. He had to talk to someone. This was not what he was expecting.

NOTES

Plasma pulse vs. ballistic weapons. Plasma weapons require additional components so are therefore heavier. This type of armament is reserved for larger rifles and other weapons platforms. Their primary use is aboard starships, drawing much of the required energy from Antaere-style gravity generators. The standard ballistic round weapon is used....

- *Introduction to Modern Weaponry*, Author: John Bear Ross, 2078,
- Amazon Kindle edition, $3.99 AD.

17

With hardly a deep breath, the three REVs reached Hut Four and barreled through the west side entrance. They were laughing, enjoying the physical exercise of the run.

The hut was of typical Quonset design; a long, half-round structure made of corrugated metal. Inside was a general-purpose room, with a spine corridor leading back to the head and showers. Along the corridor were doors to the twenty individual rooms.

Two men in black and gray utilities jumped up from the couches, startled by the sudden arrival of Zac and the others.

"What the hell's wrong with you?" Gunnery Sergeant Donovan Ross cried out. "You could give a man a heart attack."

The moment passed, and soon the five REVs were shaking hands and man-hugging. Zac couldn't remember the last time this many REVs were in one room. It was certainly a sign that things were changing.

After things settled down, they sat on the couches, clutching beers drawn from the refrigerator along the wall.

"How long have you been here?" Mike Brickey asked the two new members of the team.

"Three days," answered Kyle Johnson. He was the youngest of the group; a twenty-nine-year-old sergeant from Green Bay, Wisconsin. He had gone over ten years in the REV program only a couple of months before, becoming the newest member of the *Charlies*. The fact that he was here told Zac that the production of natural NT-4 was determined by the individual, and not so much by how long they were on the drug. That was interesting. It meant there may be more than the 351-Cs producing their own version of NT-4. He was sure Dr. Cross was already salivating over the possibilities.

"Did they tell you anything else?" Zac asked.

The faces of the two new REVs turned serious. "Yeah, Patel told us."

"Arnie's here?" Zac asked.

"Yeah; he's running the hospital."

Zac was glad to hear his friend was in the camp, but it was the possibility that Olivia was with him that excited him most. That would be almost too much to expect.

"Is it true, gunny? Are we really producing our own NT-4?" asked Donovan Ross.

"It's true," Angus Price answered for him. "And it's not *Gunnery Sergeant* Murphy anymore, but *Second Louie* Murphy."

All eyes turned to the newly-minted officer. "I didn't ask for this," Zac pleaded.

"But you didn't turn it down, either."

Zac waved his hand, as if dismissing the subject. "Listen up guys. I think we need to face reality. We're a new breed of REV that no one knows what to do with. At this point they say they want to turn us into a team of super REVs—"

"For what missions...sir?" Kyle interrupted, followed by a wide grin.

"Unknown, but it can't be what we've been used to. We're unique, but I don't think the brass know how much at this point."

"What do you mean?"

Zac had already discussed this with Angus and Mike during the trip to Camp Slater. Now he told the others about his experiences on Eliza-3 and the discovery of on-call cascading to boost even his naturally-superior abilities. It was like a surge of adrenalin, but with more than just the energy. Along with it came, strength, awareness and even mental capacity. The others—including Angus and Mike—hadn't experienced the cascading before, and if they had, they didn't see it for what it was. Zac was convinced it was something he could control, at least in times of stress or physical activity. But like anything, it took practice. Camp Slater—Zac believed—was designed to explore the limits of their natural abilities. After that, the missions would be tailored to their unique talents.

After a little more discussion and reminiscing, Zac dismissed the team so they could claim rooms in the barracks and get some chow. A schedule was posted by the front door of the barracks, starting the next day. Today was reserved for settling in.

Zac went next door to the hospital hoping to run into an old friend.

The hospital was essentially a large tent with dozens of sectioned off compartments. There wasn't much going on inside, not yet.

The bulk of the REVs had only just arrived. Tomorrow the work of the medical staff would begin.

He asked if Dr. Patel was in the building and told he wasn't. He asked about Olivia next.

"I believed she and a couple of the nurses headed over to the mess hall a few minutes ago."

He walked next door.

The mess hall took up half of Hut Five; the other half was the galley. The compliment of the base was small, so the mess was too, with only a dozen tables with bench seating. Zac spotted Olivia the moment he entered.

She noticed him, too, and rose from the table to rush to him. They shared a respectable familiarity hug, which still evoked a series of giggles and catcalls from the table of females.

"Let's go outside," she said to Zac.

When the door swung close, the greeting was much more passionate.

"I knew this time was coming," Olivia said between sniffles. "We've been preparing for your arrival for three weeks."

"Really? I was still on Eliza-3."

"I know, they told us."

"I want to thank you by the way," Zac said with feeling. "The gift you smuggled to me saved my life."

"Oh you got it! Thank god, I wasn't sure."

The Marine survival kit had been a godsend.

Zac's mood turned sour. "So Cross is here, too?"

"He comes and goes; It's mainly me and Arnie." Then she smiled. "Along with some of the cutest nurses and therapists I've ever seen. You guys should have a lot of fun while you're here, if you're allowed to fraternize."

Zac pulled her tight. "I've got your frantanization right here."

"And impressive it is…Lieutenant Murphy. Yes, I heard. Congratulations."

"We'll see how it goes. Congratulations may not be in order." He looked past her to the door of the hut. "Let's go back inside and make your friends jealous. I'm starving."

"So am I." She grabbed his ass. "But for something I can't get in the mess hall."

"Don't be so sure."

NOTES

An interesting development. We've been observing a marked increase in our subject's physical strength and other functions even when not activated. David and I agree this is a side effect of the residual NT-4 in the system. I understand the need for the residual for the survivability of the subject at their heightened metabolic levels, but could this mean the REVs, as they're calling themselves, can remain in control and with added abilities? That was the original goal of the NT program. My fingers are crossed.

- Journal Entry, June 6, 2073, Dr. Clifford Slater

18

At oh-six-thirty the next morning, Zac and his men were dressed in sweats and tennis shoes, ready to begin the first day of becoming *real* Marines, according to Bull Bullock.

They went to the hospital before eating and had monitors hooked up to them and blood drawn. This was how every day was to begin. Zac caught up briefly with Arnie Patel. Neither spoke about the incident back on the *Olympus*. Zac was ready to put it behind him. He was beginning a new chapter in his life. It was better to move on…if people would let him. Patel was more than willing.

After breakfast, the team met in the farthest hut along the line, number eight. It was a small gym, with weight equipment, ropes dangling from the ceiling and thick mats on the floor. Bullock was there, along with a fit-looking man in bare feet, stretching and practicing spin kicks.

"Welcome to the first day of the rest of your miserable lives," said Bull. He already had a thin sheen of sweat on his skin from an early-morning workout. "Here's where we begin to teach you how to defend yourself. I don't know your individual level of physical conditioning, but I'm going to find out. Any slackers are going to get extra duty until you can stand with the rest of your team. Now let's get started. Mister Murphy, front and center."

Zac stepped onto the mat.

"This is Sergeant Andy Copeland, two-time All-Marine Martial Arts Champion. He will be your combat instructor. Pay attention. If you don't, you'll get a cracked skull or broken ribs. Command will be pissed if that happens and I'll get my ass chewed out. You don't want command to chew my ass. Sergeant…."

"Mister Murphy," Copeland began. "I want to start slow, and with just enough to prove my credentials. In any form of training, respect for your instructor is important. Now, I'm going to slip around you, using some basic foot movements designed to evade an attacker's blows. See if you can hit me."

"You want me to hit you?"

Copeland smiled. "I want you to *try* to hit me."

Zac looked at his fellow REVs. They didn't look amused. They knew what was coming.

The martial arts expert began bobbing and weaving, while tracing a circle around Zac with balanced and practiced steps. Zac watched the man, turning slowly with the movements. REVs brains operate on a different level than other people. The drug of their namesake also gave them the instincts of a chase animal, complete with intense concentration and an ability to follow movements with unnatural focus. It wasn't that they saw the enemy movements in slow motion, it was that their brains were working at a faster pace. They reacted quicker, which also translated into faster response times for their own movements.

In a flash, Zac lashed out with a left fist, striking Copeland square on the nose. From Zac's superior strength, the man fell flat on his back unconscious, his nose broken and bleeding.

Bull dropped down to him, cradling his head, checking his pulse. There were two other assistants standing nearby. The master sergeant told them to get a medic.

"What the fuck was that?" he yelled up at Zac.

"He told me to hit him."

"Not to nearly kill him!"

"Sorry. I didn't know how hard it would be. I've never hit anyone other than a Qwin before, and that was always to kill." Zac didn't tell the instructor that he also didn't know how it *felt* to hit a Qwin. He had no recollection, just the photographic memory of it happening.

Copeland was coming to, struggling to sit up as one of the assistants placed a rag over his bleeding nose and mouth. He was too dazed to hold the rag himself.

"What…what happened?" he asked.

"A REV happened," Mike Brickey said. "That's what."

After the self-defense fiasco, Bull set the REVs to a weightlifting exhibition, not so much for conditioning but to get some idea just how strong the REVs were. He began with himself, pressing two-hundred eighty-five pounds with relative ease.

Zac told him his men didn't need weight training, but Bull insisted. Angus was the first up. He lifted the two-eighty-five without even a groan. The sergeant moved it up to three-twenty-five. Again, not even a grunt.

"Here, let's get this over with," said Donovan. He set the weight at six hundred pounds. These weren't free weights, but set on a machine, so Bull didn't protest the impossible lift.

Angus struggled but lifted the weight. Bull stood with his mouth open, stunned into silence. Angus sat up for a moment, a look of shock on his face, as well. But his was different. It was a look of revelation. He lay back down and pushed on the bar again. It rose up, taking the impossible load with it. Then he lifted again…and again. After a five lift set, he sat up on the bench.

"I felt it!"

Zac frowned.

"Felt what?" Bull asked, recovering from his stupor.

Angus had caught Zac's warning. "You know…the rush. This is fun. Let's do some more."

Bull looked at the rest of the team. "Can all of you do that?"

Shy grins and nods answered him.

The sergeant major shook his head. "This is ridiculous. Let's do something that requires skill and not just brute force. I guess what they say about you guys is right; brawn and no brains."

Zac didn't take offense. The man was just feeling insecure at the moment. Who could blame him?

After lunch, the team met up with Bull on the firing range.

There were several long-distance sniper stations set up with mean-looking long-barrel rifles set on low tripods. There was a station for each of the REVs, plus Bullock, with an enlisted man assigned to each. Zac scanned the horizon for the targets. They were barely visible.

"Now here's something that requires skill," said Bull Bullock. He knelt down and placed a huge hand on the weapon at his station. "This is the Nance One-Twenty-Two air-cooled full charge pulse rifle. Where other version fire plasma bolts, for our lesson today these will be firing ballistic slugs, seven-point-two caliber, full-metal jacket. Do any of you know what any of that means?"

Zac had to admit, he didn't. During his fifteen years as a REV, he had used a variety of weapons, but always those integrated into his armor. His training consisted of hours upon mindless hours of pointing and shooting, to the point it became instinctive. That was the point. During a Run everything had to be instinctive. A REV didn't think. Until now.

"I'm familiar with some of the terms," said Donovan Ross. "Me and my buddies did a lot of shooting when I was a kid in Texas. It's just what we did."

"Anything like this?"

"Nope. But it's still a rifle."

"Then please, Gunnery Sergeant Ross, take a position."

Donovan settled in, placing the stock firmly against his shoulder and sighting through the computerized scope.

"Whenever you're ready."

A low-tone blast sounded, rumbling away across the desert. A set of monitors were placed behind each station. Everyone turned to see the result of the shot at the target over a mile-and-a-half away.

It was a hit, on the lower right corner of the target; a plastic square with concentric circles and a small 'x' in the middle.

"Not bad, sergeant. Not bad at all. It that were a Qwin you would have shot off his left pinkie. Good for you. He won't be using that finger anymore."

Bull looked at Zac. The man obviously had it out for him. There was always one in every group who received the bulk of the DI's attention. It was Zac's turn.

"Have you had any experience shooting, other than through your so-called REV training."

There it was again, that attitude about REVs.

"None, sergeant major."

Bull smiled. "Then please, take a station."

Zac lay down on the mat next to Bullock's station. He felt awkward as he moved his body against the weapon. It seemed a lot larger, more intimidating, than it did a moment before. Now he tried to get all his parts in sync with the rifle.

"Shoulder firm into the stock," Bull instructed, taking a more professional tone. "Rest your cheek along the barrel, sight through the scope, but not too close. Keep both eyes open."

The magnified image wobbled as he took control of the weapon, losing sight of the target completely. He finally got the distant object in the scope again, finding that he could controlled the rifle from the rear, not the front, as it swiveled on the tripod. Now it was beginning to make sense.

Bullock was looking at the monitor behind Zac. "You got it?" he asked.

"Yep."

"You see the targeting dot? That's how the scope is set up. It's computerized, and takes into account the distance, the drop, temperature, humidity, even the rotation of the planet. You can recalibrate more precisely after a shot by marking the hit and then moving a second dot to center target. Take your time, Mister Murphy. Fire when ready."

Zac looked through the scope. The target board nearly filled his vision, but not completely, making the tiny 'x' barely visible from this distance, even through the scope. Being able to see what Donovan saw, Zac thought it a miracle that he hit any part of the target at all. But now it was Zac's turn to concentrate.

Another feature of being a REV was the acuteness of their eyesight. They could see about twice as far and clear as a normal person, and that was without cascading. Zac was relying on the natural magnification of the scope, along with all its fancy gizmos. Now he began to rely on himself.

He really wanted to make a good shot, and the stress of the desire worked its way into his brain, just as he hoped. The image in the scope seemed to brighten as Zac's attention became more focused. As he concentrated on the distant 'x', the more it seemed to grow in size, to the point where it filled almost his entire vision. He could even see tiny threads of ink along the edges of the printing.

The targeting dot was lined up on the 'x'. Zac squeezed the trigger.

"A hit!" Kyle called out as he studied the monitor.

Zac was confused. The 'x' was still there, with no evidence of a hit.

"Very good, Mister Murphy. Impressive…for a first attempt."

Zac twisted around until he could see the monitor. A flashing round circle indicated a spot below the black circles and to the left, but still on the target board.

"A balls shot," Bullock said. "No more nookie for Mr. Qwin."

Zac turned back to the scope. He relaxed his focus, allowing the image to pull back until he could see the whole target and the hole from his first shot. He reached up and used a small toggle bar to move a second targeting dot to the hole. He pressed the end of the lever, locking in the position. Then he worked the control until another dot lined up with the 'x'. He pressed the lever again.

"That's it, Mr. Murphy," said Bullock. "Let's get on with the lesson."

"In a minute," Zac replied. He gripped the weapon, familiar now with the recoil. His eyes focused on the 'x'. The image in his mind grew larger….

The next shot was dead center on the 'x'. There were gasps

from the spectators and cheers from the REVs. But now that the target was dialed in, Zac wasn't through. He fired again.

There was silence behind him. "Did he miss?" someone asked.

"No, look, the circle's flashing. He sent it right through the same hole!"

Zac fired three more times, sending each round through the hole he made with his first.

When he was done, he leaned over on his left shoulder and looked up at Bull Bullock. "I'm ready for my lesson now, sergeant major."

Over the next two weeks it was the same story.

Tactic assault maneuvers: One look at the hand signals and the REVs had them down. They were also faster, with quicker reactions and could jump twice as high. They moved to the targets with the speed and fluidity of a ballet, each piece working in perfect harmony.

Close Quarters Combat: With their superior eye-to-hand coordination and accelerated decision making, the REVs aced the friend-foe test in record time. In fact, they began to compete against each other to see who could run the course the fastest without an error. Zac was disappointed that he came in second behind Kyle, but only by a fraction of a second. They were *all* within a fraction of a second from each other.

Hand-To-Hand Combat: They never returned to this drill again after Copeland was airlifted out of the Camp. Zac tried to feel sorry for the man, but he couldn't. The martial arts *expert* would live with the lesson that REVs were pretty tough hombres, even when not activated.

The only real challenge Zac and his men faced were space operations. Although REVs could be used to assault enemy spacecraft, it was rarely done. When they did, it involved the use of a boarding vessel and a mini Run within the confines of the ship. The REV would be in an armored spacesuit to protect against pressure loss. These Runs usually lasted only a couple of minutes. After a few hull punctures there wasn't much left after that.

But this was different. They were being trained in small, pilot-controlled pods to approach a ship, make contact and gain entrance, sometimes covertly, other times with direct assaults. They would shuttle up to a waiting star cruiser where the exercises would initiate. Several types of ships were brought in for them to play with. And that's how the REVs felt about the training. Of all the drills they were being put through, this was the most thrilling and challenging. It was a blast playing *Luke Skywalker* in their little pods.

And that's how Zac's first two weeks at Camp Slater were spent…and least during the day.

Olivia had been right. There was an overabundance of attractive women on the base, if that was possible. Clearly sixty percent of the personnel were female, and each one was a looker, physically fit, smart and attentive. Although Zac concentrated on only one of them, the other four REVs didn't discriminate or hold back. It was a miracle that even men with the physical conditioning of a REV could still have any energy left for the next day's drills.

And that was the routine: Sexual escapades most of the night, with drilling of a different kind during the day. And the drills weren't so much training than just repetitive exercises, almost like REV training—real REV training.

But Zac couldn't fault the instructors. There wasn't a task

they were given that the REVs didn't ace. This was something new to the bulk of the Marines on the base. All they knew of REVs was the image of the mad killing machines with super Human strength and endurance during a Run. Very few people knew the truth; that REVs retained a portion of their super-human abilities even when not on a Run.

But how could they know the truth? REVs weren't allowed to socialize with the average Marine or civilian. They lived in their own sections of a base or starship and ate in special sections in the mess halls. They didn't need to work out or join other Marines in sporting events. The only interaction came mainly with females, and that was also closely regulated. Thinking back, Zac and Olivia had never gone on a date, and all the times they got together it was in his compartment. Sometimes she would fix dinner—or get it from the mess decks—and bring it to him. They would share a candle-lit dinner…before hopping in the sack.

Since his time on Eliza-3, Zac had been doing a lot of thinking about his time in the Corps and what he sacrificed to become a REV. It made his new reality even more precious and eye opening.

REVs were not allowed off the base or to take liberty. When his parents would come to visit, it was on the base and under watch. It was as if he was in prison. The more he thought about it, the more the description fit. Then it really hit home when he realized he hadn't driven a car in fourteen years.

This wasn't to say REVs didn't stay occupied. It's just that they had so little time that wasn't taken up with preparing for a Run or recovering from one. Zac did read books and watch movies—in his compartment. As a kid he used to write, and for the first few years as a REV he kept a journal. But then the stories became redundant. It was the same thing over and over. He put his journals away and never returned to them.

Occasionally, Zac would pull up his bank account on the computer. He was a wealthy man, according to what others said. And he should be, after fifteen years of spending essentially no money. The Corps provided for his every need. He didn't have to pay for anything.

This had been his life for fifteen years. A life of routine, a life of Rev.

But that had all changed four short months ago.

Zac took a walk in the cool night air of the desert, gazing up at strange constellations which probably included Sol in one of them. He didn't know; that wasn't something he'd taken the time to find out. Maybe now he would. He'd traveled the stars, so maybe astronomy wouldn't be such a bad hobby to have….

He laughed out loud. He'd never had a hobby before, at least not in his adult life. Now he was realizing there were a lot of things he hadn't done. And having a life was one of them.

The frustration—even anger—returned. Although part of him was still proud of his time as a REV—a regular REV—he could see now how he'd been sold a bill of goods. Fifteen years of his life was gone. He wondered what the next fifteen would bring. He was resolved to make it fuller, more satisfying, more…normal.

For the first time he could remember, he was anxious to see what the dawn would bring.

NOTES

WAR! As has been chronicled in countless science fictions stories and movies, mankind is now at war with a race of space aliens. As implausible as that sounds, it is a reality. It was also inevitable. That is just what we do as a race: we fight. And if it's not against our own kind, then why not against aliens? However, this time it may not be humanity that comes out on top.

- Editorial, New York Times, July 9, 2077

19

Brigadier General Bill Smith lit a cigar, drew in the sweet smoke and leaned his head back to shoot a roiling cloud toward the ceiling of his office.

"You know it cost over four hundred adjusted-dollars to have just one of these things shipped out here," he said to Zac. "You want one?"

"I never acquired the taste, sir. But you go right ahead."

Smith smiled, scanning the newly-minted lieutenant with his steel-blue eyes. "How you liking the bar?"

"Never thought much about it until now, sir. Rank doesn't matter when you're a REV. We had a singular job to do and just about any of us could do it."

"Doesn't sound like you were challenged much."

"Surviving a Run was enough. Everything after that was bonus."

Smith nodded and put the stogie in a well-used ashtray on his desk. "So how's your team shaping up?"

Zac knew the base commander received constant updates on

his team of super REVs. "Just fine, sir. We're acing every task put before us, and no offense, but things are getting kind of *redundant* with all the drills and exercises."

Zac prided himself on the use of the word *redundant*, rather than *boring*. It seemed like something an officer might say.

"You think your men are up for a real challenge, something to test their mettle as a team?"

Zac's heart jumped. He was hoping this was the reason for the meeting.

"I'd say we're more than ready, general. We're used to going on missions every month or so. We've been here for two already, and that's not counting the time I spent on Eliza-3. For one, I'm ready for some action. What's the op?"

A quick slash-and-burn operation would be just what he and his men needed.

"Don't be so anxious, lieutenant, not until you've heard the details."

The general took another long drag off the cigar then clipped off the tip, saving the rest for later. He took out a datapad and turned it on.

"Have you ever heard of the Temple of Light on ES-3, a planet called Iz'zar?"

"Of course; it's one of the Antaere Big Five religious sites. It's supposed to be one huge mother, as well."

"It's actually ranked their second most-sacred Temple, behind only the Temple of Order on Antara. Anything else you know about it?"

"You'll have to forgive me, general, but as a REV, I was never too interested in the history behind our targets, or the politics, either. As they say, we're wound up, pointed in a direction and let go."

Smith nodded. He'd worked many an op with REVs in his career. He knew their strengths, along with their weaknesses.

"Then let me tell you about it," he began. "Even though the Temple's been a juicy target for decades, we've never dared take it out. Hell, I doubt we even could if we wanted to. Being so sacred to the Order, if we destroyed it, it would be like taking out the Statue of Liberty, or those buildings back at the beginning of the century in New York. It would piss off a lot of people and for no strategic value."

"You want us to take it out?" Zac asked, half-kidding.

"Don't jump the gun, lieutenant," Smith said. "That is *not* what we want you to do." Using his datapad, the general activated a monitor on the wall to his right. A picture of the huge domed structure came up, which cross-faded to others, most taken at a distance, before shifting to a graphic showing connecting lines in space above the planet.

"Consider this, Mr. Murphy: Multiple layers of space-based shielding to protect against orbital attack." The image changed to show radiating lines penetrating the ground around the complex. "Electrodes embedded around the entire structure to a mile deep to prevent tunneling." The next slide showed row upon row of yellow-skinned aliens armed with their K-2 assault weapons. "Add to that twenty thousand Antaere troops within the walls, along with a quarter-million fanatical natives outside the complex, all trained in defense of the Temple. Hell, even a hundred REVs couldn't make a dent in the place. And there aren't enough Marines in the Corps to mount an effective ground assault. Couple all that with the shitstorm that would result if we attacked such a religious site, and you have a truly invulnerable fortress."

Zac had once been a senior NCO before putting on his lieutenant's hardware. He was also the top REV in the Corps, as well as borderline super-Human. So even though Bill Smith was a general, Zac wasn't intimidated by the man. He stared up at the ceiling, catching the general's attention.

"What are you looking at?"

"The anvil, sir. Just waiting for it to drop."

Smith smiled. "Relax, lieutenant. Those things take time to hoist up, and then they have to be released at the precise moment for the most impact."

"That's what I'm afraid of…sir."

Smith continued, a thin smile on his face: "Another question. Have you ever heard of the Book of Order?"

"Yes sir, it's the Antaere Bible, Quran and Kabala all rolled up in one."

"Exactly. Now what about the Corollaries? Have you heard of them?"

"That I have not."

"They're a set of supplements to the Book of Order which spell out specific instructions on how to achieve the universal order the book strives to teach." Smith put finger quotes around the words *universal order*. "They're only viewed by the Antaere, and very few people outside the Order even know they exist. But there is one in particular that's most interesting. It's called the Final Glory."

"Why is that one so interesting?"

"Because it is rumored to detail the Antaere plans for their alien worshippers."

"In what way, sir?"

"According to inside sources we've only recently gained access to, the text instructs the Antaere to first *use* the aliens for power and material gain…and then to *kill* them, supposedly leaving the Antaere as the only advanced species in the galaxy. Of course, at this point we're only talking about the Grid.

There's still a lot of the galaxy that hasn't been explored yet, but you get the idea."

"They want to kill their followers? That doesn't make any sense."

"It doesn't say when this will happen, just that that's their intention, their Final Glory, as they call it. Now how do you think half-a-trillion loyal worshippers would react knowing this news?"

"I imagine they wouldn't be too happy. There's even a small, but fanatical, sect still back on Earth. I think we're the only place in the Grid that allows open worship of their religion on a non-Antaere world."

"Command thinks they'll go ballistic, throwing away their loyalty to the Antaere and setting up a scenario where we can win this war once and for all."

Zac studied the photos as they appeared on the monitor. "What does this have to do with the Temple of Light?"

"There are only two known copies of the Corollaries. One is on Antara, the other is on ES-3."

"In the Temple?"

"In the Temple."

"It would be nice to get our hands on that document." Zac said. "So what do you have in mind, general? You just said the place is impenetrable."

"That's where the challenge comes in, Mr. Murphy."

"Did the anvil just come crashing down?" Zac was shaking his head. "General, we just put this team together, made up of very unique individuals, and now you want us to go on a suicide mission? We may have enhanced abilities, but against twenty thousand Qwin and a quarter million loyal natives, even activated we couldn't pull that off. Isn't there something a little less… impossible we could do?"

Smith leaned back in his chair, studying Zac's reaction. "Would you like to hear the details?"

Details? The man actually has details on how to pull off an impossible mission.

"Of course, sir. I'm all ears."

"As I said, the complex is invulnerable to outside attack. That's why we're going to smuggle you and your team in on an Antaere starship. Then once inside, you'll proceed to the Enlightenment Chamber, where we believe the document is kept."

"You believe? How good is your intel?"

"The Enlightenment Chamber is where all the important documents are stored. It's only accessible by the High Priests, and they go there often to view the ancient texts and to study other writings."

"And this Corollary thing is there?"

"All the Corollaries are there, including the Final Glory."

"Assuming we can get that far, won't this be one of the most heavily-guarded documents of the Antaere race?"

"The priests study these documents daily. The Enlightenment Chamber is essentially a small library, and it would be impractical for them to keep everything under lock and key within the room. Once inside, it should be yours for the taking."

"Once inside? Okay, how do we do *that*?"

Smith grimaced. "There's the rub, lieutenant. We can get you only so far, after that your special abilities come into play. You'll have to adapt, improvise, and overcome."

"Literally, sir."

"That's right. And one other thing: You'll have to get into the Enlightenment Chamber without anyone knowing you're there. If they learn of your mission before you reach it, they'll destroy the document to keep us from letting the cat out of the bag."

Zac's REV brain was working overtime, almost to the point

where he felt his body cascading a little, getting a boost with the processing.

"So in summary, general: Somehow we arrive at the Temple in an Antaere starship, sneak into the second most-holy site the aliens have, locate a secure room which we have no idea where it is, break in and steal the most super-secret document they have." He hesitated, watching the general's face for any signs this was just a big practical joke. There was none. "And then there's the question of extraction. I assume there won't be a massive recovery effort if we get the text?"

"We've made contact with some of the resistance outside the Temple. They'll be ready to get you into space for a pick up. But, lieutenant, this is where the fun comes in."

Zac didn't say a word. He leaned back in his chair, confused by the surreal tone of the briefing.

"After you get possession of the document, how you get out of the Temple is up to you," Smith said, seriously. "If it takes all of your special REV abilities to do so—along with a shitload of alien bodies—then so be it. Once we have the document, we can weather the ridicule by revealing its contents, saying we did all this to protect you—you poor, gullible creatures—from the killer Antaere."

"When do you expect to launch the operation?"

"Seventy-two hours from now."

Zac's mouth fell open. "Sir, that's not enough time. It will take weeks, even months of planning. It takes longer than that to layout a REV Run."

Smith smiled, this time a wicked, inside-joke kind of smile. "What do you think you've been doing here for the past three months?"

"Sir?"

"The assault obstacles you've been running are an accurate

layout of the ground between the Temple spaceport and the main complex. And the Close Quarters Combat drills have been for when you enter the building and make your way to the Enlightenment Chamber. And the exercises in space have been to train you to gain access to the Antaere starship. Lieutenant Murphy, you're team *is* ready."

It took another hour for the general to brief Zac on the finer details of the operation. After that, he returned to the barracks to break the news to his men. When he did, there was a flood of questions, many of which Zac couldn't answer, some he could.

"What the hell is a *whippet?*" asked Angus Price.

"From what I understand, it's a pair of co-joined pods that whip each other through space using kinetic energy instead of chemical fuel."

"And we're supposed to use these to do what?"

"To position ourselves behind the Qwin starship before it reengages its gravity drive."

"And then we just get sucked along at faster-than-light speed over six light-years, outside the ship, in outer space? I didn't know that was possible."

Zac pulled up the diagram on the datapad, copying it to the devices each member of the team was holding. "We won't be exposed; we'll be in these pods. They're like ejection capsules, so we should feel right at home."

No one was buying it, and Zac didn't blame them. When General Smith explained it to him, he had the same reaction.

The crown-prince of the Antaere—something called the *Rowin* in Qwin-speak—was scheduled to visit the temple on Iz'zar sometime over the next three weeks. Once his ship and heavy escort passed through a section of space, spies would report and Zac's team would move into position behind the aliens. A small Human fleet would then attack from the front, requiring the ship carrying the prince to be moved to the rear for safe keeping until the outcome of the battle could be determined. That's where Zac and his REVs would be waiting. Then the Humans would break off their frontal attack, allowing the prince to continue with his journey.

By then, Zac and his team will have whipped their way behind the Qwin ship, leaving no chemical exhaust trail to detect. Their positioning had to be precise when the gravity well was created, otherwise they would slip past the starship and into the miniature singularity. But if things went according to plan, the team would move up to the aft section of the royal starship and blend their small pods with a series of matching static electricity nullifiers attached to the hull. Theoretically, no one would notice the extra cylinders within the dual arches of ten. Only if someone counted the pods would they suspect something was amiss.

After that, the REVs would each receive a dose of Twilight to knock them out for the five-day duration of the trip. It was explained that only REVs could handle the drug and come out at the other end fully revived and aware. All the other people they'd tested were in a stupor for up to twenty-four hours after coming off the drug. That wouldn't do for this mission. Instead, Zac's people would essentially go into suspended animation, without need for food and with only minimal life support. They'd awake at their destination ready for action.

The alien starship was the only one that could land at the

Temple Complex without extensive inspection and security. After all, this was the Rowin's ship; he would receive immediate clearance.

Once on the ground, the team would leave their pods and make their way into the main Temple building.

Zac had to laugh. General Smith and the geniuses back on Earth had detailed plans for how the team would gain access to the Temple Complex...or at least the spaceport on the grounds. They also had a pretty good idea how to get them off the planet after the op; using the natives who sided with the Humans. What was missing was everything in between. That was up to Zac and his team to figure out.

Fortunately, much of the guesswork only lasted for half the mission. As the general explained, once Zac had the document, they could use whatever means necessary to make their escape, even if it meant razing the Temple to the ground. Zac liked that part of the mission, even though Smith emphasized time and again that that option was only a last resort. Stealth was the name of the game.

The problem: Zac and his men were REVs. Stealth was not in their lexicon, or at least it hadn't been until they changed. It would be interesting to see how long they lasted before resorting to old habits.

This time when Zac and Olivia parted, they were able to say goodbye. He wasn't allowed to tell her about the mission, so he shrugged it off as just a little shakedown op for him and his team, nothing serious.

Then they boarded a fast transport ship for a region of space deep within Antaere territory. They traveled unescorted to avoid detection and arrived five days later. The area was within a thin nebula through which starships had to skirt dangerous clouds of thicker gas to avoid overloading their gravity wells. There was one particular transit route narrower than most where the team would lay in wait. Passive spy vessels, each manned by a single Marine, were stationed along the channel, waiting for the tell-tale sign of a passing fleet of starships.

The prince would be escorted by a thirty-ship entourage. A slightly smaller squadron of Human ships was stationed at the end of the nebula run.

A day after arriving on station, it was reported that the Rowin had departed Antara and was on his way. Zac wondered about the source of this information; Earth had never had very good contacts on the planet or within the Antaere race. They were too unified in their fanatical religion to be turned. But somewhere a crack had been found, and the Humans were exploiting it for all it was worth.

Zac was finally playing cards with his buddies—something his REV notoriety had prevented him from doing—killing time, waiting for word of the Rowin's passing. They knew the average speed of the fleet escorting the prince, as well as the general route he would take. That provided them with a pretty good idea when the operation would commence, at least down to the day.

And today was that day.

A Navy second-class rushed into the common room. "Sir, message coming through."

Zac gave his team a quick glance then followed the petty officer to the bridge.

"Fleet detected passing grid section forty-eight, coordinates one-one-eight-four. Second detection made at one-one-nine-six. Track buster. I repeat, track buster," the voice on the speaker reported.

Zac rubbed shoulders with an ensign at the nav station as he leaned over the screen. A red dot was flashing. "We're a tenth light out," said the man. "We can get you within about forty thousand miles to the track, but I wouldn't risk getting any closer. You'll have to use the K-90's after that."

K-90 was the official designation for the whippet ships, two individual survival pods connected by a thousand-mile long cord. Zac was stumped over how they worked but was assured they did.

"How long will it take you to get us into position?"

"Forty, fifty minutes, after that it's up to the whippets. After the Antaere ship arrives on station you'll have to adjust your position manually. We'll keep the support ships busy until you do."

"Thank you, Mr. Graves."

"Good luck, sir."

NOTES

With the start of the war, the military has taken over my program. They've even assigned me a new assistant, a liaison they call him. First Lieutenant David Cross, M.D. At least he's a doctor, a research scientist formerly with the CDC. I saw this coming. But now…more funding! Can't complain too much.

- Journal Entry, April 15, 2078, Dr. Clifford Slater

20

In the launch bay of the Navy starship, Zac surveyed his team and the outfits they wore. He tried hard not to laugh.

It was fortunate that Humans and the Antaere were of similar size and build; this was the result of evolving on essentially identical worlds, the quintessential ES planets. So the planners back on Earth decided that it was best if Zac and his team go in disguise, wearing full-body uniforms of a particular class of Qwin technician. These were space-drive engineers who needed special gear laced with damping wires and circuits to protect them against the ravages of the intensive magnetic fields the engines created. The outfits were made of a flexible composite material, gray in color with diagonal yellow stripes running across the chest. They looked like gaudy leotards, form-fitting and leaving nothing to the imagination. The team wore restrictive undergarments to hide the obvious differences between the two species; even then the uniforms were ugly and awkward to wear.

They also had full-head, pullover masks, with built in goggles which would hide their faces. Gloves would conceal the pink skin of the Humans.

The question Zac had for General Smith was how would the Qwin react to a group of starship crewmembers traipsing through their most-sacred Temple still wearing their work uniforms while off the ship? He didn't have an answer, except that Zac and his people should act like they belong there. That and carry a clipboard. No one ever questioned someone carrying a clipboard.

And as for weapons?

Each team member would carry a small, hard-sided backpack containing a collapsible M-101 assault rifle with shortened barrel and suppressor, along with an HK-14 handgun with 24-round magazines—six each. There would also be a change of uniform and a set of light armor that could be placed over sensitive areas of their bodies, just in case. Since the spandex-like outfits had no place to conceal the weapons, they would have to access them from the backpacks on the fly and only when needed. General Smith kept emphasizing that the weapons were only there as backups, since the mission called for stealth access of the Enlightenment Chamber. After that, Zac and his men were expected to use on-site resources for the remainder of the mission.

"Five days in these things," Mike Brickey commented. "I feel like I want to do a pirouette in this getup, more than assault an alien stronghold."

"And you would be graceful beyond belief," said Kyle Johnson. The two men locked arms and spun around a couple of times.

"Glad to see you're all in good spirits," said Zac. He could feel the strange release of tension himself, incongruous considering the impossible mission they were about to embark upon.

But they were REVs and used to embarking on impossible missions. It felt good to be back in action again.

"Okay, men, saddle up."

The pod Zac was placed into was of the same design as the small assault vessels they trained in at Camp Slater. They were larger than the REV ejection capsules by about half, with control panels running along both sides of the form-fitting bed for guidance and control. But the units back at Camp Slater had been used simply for approach and entry drills, without any special add-ons. The whippet units would be attached to the pods by thick brackets lining the front side, meaning as they spun—or more correctly whipped—the g-forces would be focused behind them, pressing their bodies deeper into the specially-designed cushions. That was fine by Zac; he'd made over a hundred landings under similar conditions. However, this time he wouldn't be under the influence of any of the pre-drugs to help with the forces he would experience. They were counting on cascading to provide the team with what they needed to survive the forces involved.

The team would break away from the whippet at some point and manually pilot the pods to the alien starship. A piece of cake.

Each member of the team was locked into their pods. Zac and Mike would be one set, Donovan and Kyle in another, with Angus balanced out by an unmanned pod carrying their weapons packs. When all was ready, the pod pairs were moved into a magnetic launch tube. The incredibly long cables were already outside the ship with automated tether hooks waiting for the signal to lock on.

"Cutting internal gravity," a voice said from speakers within his capsule. "Preparing to deploy pods. T-minus five seconds, four, three, two...."

Zac felt the queasiness that came with the loss of gravity, something all people experienced as they felt like they were falling. It only lasted a second before being replaced by the more pleasant sensation of floating.

"Whippets locking," said the voice. "All systems green."

Through the viewport in his pod, Zac saw a double set of menacing-looking metal claws approach through the void of space. There were tiny lights flashing on the tips, and a moment later he heard a heavy clank as the four huge struts became anchored to his craft. He had a vague idea what was about to happen, so when a whirling sound transferred through the hull of the pod, signifying the struts were locking into position, he felt a little more secure in the process.

"Relax gentlemen," said the voice through the speakers, with almost a tinge of humor in it. "The cables will now be deployed. This will take about five minutes. After that I will give you a heads up just before the sequence begins. You'll find a comfort bag in the compartment near your right hand that can be fitted over your mouth. I would suggest you put it on while you have the chance. There is no shame in doing so."

Zac felt with his fingers until he found the compartment. Inside was an elaborate barf-bag with straps that could be fastened around his head. He closed the compartment. He knew where it was; he would wait to see if he needed it.

A few minutes later the pod was well away from the starship and seemingly hanging in space completely alone. The two-foot thick cable that was the whippet line disappeared into space after leaving the anchor struts. A thousand miles away, at the other end, Mike Brickey was resting in his own pod.

"You ready, Sergeant Brickey," he said into his comm.

"And if I said no, would you call off this crazy stunt…sir?" The team was still getting used to his new rank.

"I'm told this will be like a carnival ride. You like carnival rides, don't you, Mike?"

"Not particularly. They always—"

The conversation came to an abrupt end, replaced by an agonizing screech not unlike a REV's primal scream. Zac watched on the HUD as the graphic representation of Mike's pod raced toward his, with a thin white line connecting them. A moment later the pod shot past—at least in the graphic. It continued to move at incredible velocity, with the loop of the loose connecting line drawing ever tighter…until.

Zac was shoved back into his cushion by what felt like the weight of a dozen African elephants standing on his chest. And then the sensation got worse.

He sucked in as much air as he could into his collapsed lungs, experiencing such a rush of acceleration that he thought he would be crushed. His body cascaded, and not just a little, but enough to make him worry about losing control. Yet he was also thankful for the added energy in his body as his natural defensives fought against this new threat.

The excruciating pressure continued for what seemed like hours, when in reality it was only about a minute. Then suddenly everything returned to normal, whatever that meant. Once the acceleration stopped, his body was weightless again.

In a panic he focused on the heads-up display. His pod had stopped—relative to the other capsule—and now it was Mike's that was moving again. Suddenly, the briefing he'd received from the techs made sense. The thousand-mile-long cable was designed to stretch, but in only one direction. It would expand until the lead pod reached the end and then recoil, pulling the trailing pod forward and past the first one, until it became the lead and reached the limit of the cord. Then the process would repeat over and over. Zac had been told the speed of the whips would increase for a while, until the laws of motion slowly took over. Whippets were not perpetual-motion machines, but pretty darn close. They were so efficient in their operation that they loss very little momentum from the constant stretching and contracting of the cable. But eventually the initial energy boost from the launch would be consumed and the whips would become less-dramatic. Eventually the strange contraption would come to a stop. By then, Zac and his team will have disconnected.

But for now, Zac took the opportunity of the brief lull between whips to pull out the barf-bag and hurriedly fasten it to his head. He finished not a moment too soon, before the pod was pulled off again through space, just like a carnival ride—the one that shot its occupants into a warm summer sky using a huge sling-shot-like device.

A few seconds later, Zac was wondering how he would dispose of the rapidly filling barf-bag once all the whipping ended. It would be hell having to live with the smell for the duration of his time in the pod.

"Excuse me, Lieutenant Murphy," said the detached voice in the speakers again. "Did I neglect to give you a heads up about the first whip? Forgive me, but I'm sure you'll be pleased to hear you have reached your break-off point. The locking brackets will detach automatically. Enjoy the rest of your journey, Mister Murphy."

"Wait a minute!" Zac yelled out. "Just who the hell are you?"

"The name is Cain, sir, petty officer second class Adam

Cain." said the voice, with a verbal smirk. "Detaching now. Please maintain radio silence with command for the remainder of the mission. Over and out."

The huge set of metal claws broke away and drifted off into space. Zac maintained visual on them, as they reflected the light of the glowing red, green and yellow nebula filling the vast expanse of space surrounding the pod.

He activated the pod-to-pod comm link. "Report in. Everyone okay?"

A series of moans sounded though the speakers, interrupted by one emphatic: "Fucking-a! Let's do that again!"

It was Donovan Ross, the former rodeo cowboy from Lubbock, Texas.

"Are you crazy?" Angus asked. "I didn't get my comfort bag on in time and now my capsule is a bloody mess."

"Seriously?" Mike Brickey asked.

"No, Mike, it's just an expression. But the interior is covered in globs of yellow, smelly…stuff."

"Okay, knock it off," Zac ordered. "Form up on me. The Antaere ship should be arriving anytime. Be alert. In the meantime, see if you can find an operating manual for these pods on the shipboard computer. There must be some way to jettison waste."

"Are you speaking for the rest of us, lieutenant," Kyle Johnson asked, "or for yourself?"

"For the wellbeing of my men, of course. I came through the whips with flying colors."

"Yeah, right…sir."

"There are contacts, *Insir*," said the weapons officer.

"Identify."

"Human, numbering twenty-two."

"Intentions?" asked the ship's lead Antaere, the First Insir.

"Weapons are charging, they intend to attack."

The officer turned to his comm technician. "Inform the Rowin. Have his ship evacuated from the group. Send two escorts with it. Desnic, prepare for engagement, standard formation."

"Three ships breaking away, Captain," reported the tac officer aboard the fast-attack ship *Churchill*. "The others are forming up. Looks like our evil plan is working."

"Okay, Mister Connors, let's make it look convincing," said Navy Commander Paul Papa. "First squadron, commence your run. Shields on full, and try not to get your asses shot off. Remember, this is just for show."

A line of ten warcraft shot away from the main formation before breaking into twos, a lead and a wingman. They closed on the escort fleet, which now numbered twenty-seven after the huge VIP ship and two others moved away, back into the nebula.

The attack ships were of a delta-wing design, very similar to the Antaere ships, but about a tenth their size. The design came from the aliens, just as did gravity drive technology. Yet being Humans, modifications had been made. Choosing speed over firepower, the Human D-wings had only one weapon—a powerful plasma pulse cannon. It was meant not only to destroy enemy warcraft, but also to disrupt gravity well formation. Even if the Antaere wanted to dip back into a well and disappear, they couldn't. The Qwin had the same technology, so the battle was joined in normal space, until one or the other opponents bolted out of range or were destroyed.

Rapid pulses of energy streaked out from the Human ships, forming a brilliant line of incoming fire. The Qwin ships were ready, and the bolts slammed into energized absorption shields. Return fire raked the line of Human starships. Being smaller and relying more on speed than strong shielding, two of the buzzships fell out of the line with their shields down. Captain Papa couldn't risk keeping them in the fight. One clean energy bolt would be enough to destroy the fighters.

He held back sending in replacements. The purpose of the attack was to delay the Qwin, not to win the battle.

"Any word from Lieutenant Murphy?" he asked the comm officer.

"Yes sir; they're having trouble locating the Antaere starship."

"Why?"

"Unknown sir."

NOTES

Gravity Well: An effect of the Antaere gravity space drive involving the creation of an event horizon. The well is in fact created in all directions around the singularity. The 'well' effect is from the vantage point of the observer. Since the well is created in all direction, this tends to increase the effectiveness of the drive, causing a 'shrinking' of the distance in front of the generator as it moves through space, magnifying the effect. The result is a 'jumping' through space at many times the speed of light.

- *A Star Travel Primer,* Author: Dr. Jonathan Aronson. 2nd Edition, 2070

21

"Where the hell is it?" Zac asked no one in particular. Reports had come in informing his team that the prince's ship had left the escort fleet and entered a shallow gravity well a few moments later. It should have bolted back about a light-year and reappeared somewhere close to where the team waited. But nothing.

"Wait," said Angus Price. "I have contacts—three of them—but damn, they're about nine thousand miles away."

As the small cluster of six capsules drifted in space—five REV pods plus the one for the weapons—their momentum was helping them close on the contacts, but without setting any speed records. Each pod was equipped with canisters of compressed oxygen or methane for maneuvering. Detectors aboard starships were extremely sensitive and could pick up even minute traces of standard chemical exhaust. It would stand out like a lighthouse within the wispy clouds of the nebula, letting the aliens know they had company. The maneuvering gas in the pods was designed to mask their presence.

The problem is they only had so much gas per pod, to be used for the final approach and docking with the Rowin's ship, not for long-distance propulsion.

"Move over to me and lock on. We'll use a blast from one of the pods to get all of us moving."

"We'll need another to slow down," said Kyle.

"I know. Hopefully we'll have enough left over to make contact. Hurry, Captain Papa can't keep the Qwin tied up forever."

"Sir, they've located the royal. Distance…nine thousand miles."

"Nine thousand! How long will it take them to get there?"

"I don't have that information."

"Find out!"

Papa's job was one of balance. If he persisted with the attack, the Qwin may decide to call off the trip to Iz'zar and return to Antara. That would end the mission before it even got started. And if he broke off his attack before Murphy could dock with the royal starship, it would have the same effect. He had to give the REVs time without scaring off the Qwin.

Kyle was the geek of the team, and he did a quick calculation. "Nine thousand miles in twenty-nine minutes. If we go faster, it will take more gas to slow us down."

Zac grimaced. Twenty-nine minutes for a space battle wasn't that long, not considering the distances involved. Yet it would seem like an eternity to the Qwin, as they pondered whether or not to call off the trip. It would also be excruciatingly long for the

REVs, not knowing if their mission would be a go or an abort. He let Captain Papa in on the bad news. He wasn't happy, but told Zac he would do his best.

"What the hell are you doing?" Papa yelled through the comm.

"Sorry sir, a bolt got through."

"If we destroy too many of the escort ships, they'll turn for home and the mission will be a bust."

"I understand, sir. It won't happen again."

Papa slumped in his command chair. "That's okay, Ensign Rozoff; I know how odd this attack is playing out."

"It's okay, sir."

Already three of the escort ships had been destroyed. Six of Papa's ships had withdrawn from the line of fire, but were still intact. The Humans had pulled back out of range, as if reassessing their strategy. This could only go on for so long. Even a standoff would result in the Antaere withdrawing. They were on escort duty, not a strategic mission. It wouldn't take much for them to call it a day and simply reschedule the Rowin's trip to Iz'zar.

But there was one thing that would keep the aliens engaged.

"Ensign Rozoff," Papa said over the comm.

"Yes sir."

"I need you and Lieutenant Delarosa to prepare to abandon ship."

"Could you repeat that, sir?"

"I need the two of you to aim your ships at the enemy line and then bail out. We need to give the Qwin a victory, something to keep them in the fight. If they feel they're getting the upper hand, they'll stick around just for the thrill of killing Humans."

"We'll have to abandon ship close to their shields to make it convincing, maybe even take a few bolts on our forward screens."

"Agreed. You know you'll be out there for a while, until after the Qwin are gone?"

"Yes sir."

The unspoken truth in the conversation was that when the Qwin activated their gravity at the conclusion of the battle, the two Human pilots could be sucked into the singularities. Or they could be targeted by the Antaere ships and blasted just for sport. The odds of them being rescued was less than fifty-fifty.

"Set your run, Len," ordered Captain Papa. "And good luck."

"Thank you, sir. Lining up now. Engaging...."

Zac couldn't see the enemy ship, but he knew he was close. He watched the HUD as his small string of pods approached, the scale on the screen showing the two contacts closing at alarming speed.

"Fire your jets, Don," he said to Donovan Ross.

"It will clean me out."

"Understood."

Zac felt the rapid deceleration, which lasted only a couple a seconds. The cluster of pods was still moving, but much slower. The huge bulk of the royal starship loomed large to the right and down slightly.

The planners had taken into consideration the danger of the pods being detected not only by their maneuvering exhaust, but also by proximity scans of approaching objects, be they natural or man-made. That's why the pods were coated with a radar absorbing material that would render them virtually invisible to the scans. Even still, the original plan was for the tiny pods to approach individually, leaving even a smaller signature, rather than as a cluster. Zac had no way of knowing if his small fleet was visible to the Qwin. He would find out soon enough.

Zac now used his own supply of gas—his happened to be methane—to guide the string of pods toward the massive tail end of the Antaere starship. As was the common design, this one was also delta-shaped which meant it was a lot larger in back than in front. Scale was often distorted by the absolute clarity of space, and as they drifted closer, the sheer size of the craft became apparent.

This was a ship designed for the second-in-command of a starfaring civilization, one based on bloodlines and backed by religious authority. And it showed. The tiny pods were lost in the expanse of the superstructure, which included skyscraper-size modules and nodes attached seemingly helter-skelter along the hull. Zac's HUD identified the static electricity nullifiers which the pods had been built to mimic. During the briefings, they looked to be respectable size, consisting of arching stacks of ten cylinders each. Now in scale to the rest the ship, they were barely noticeable.

Zac's supply of methane ran out, leaving only Angus and Kyle's pods to get them into position. The weapons pod was unmanned, so it carried no supply of gas.

Again, the original plan had called for each pod to attach itself to one of two nullifier units. Now all six pods would have to attach to one. That made the possibility of them being noticed during a video inspection of the exterior hull more likely. It was a chance they had to take.

Zac checked the mission clock. It was going on thirty-five minutes since he'd told Captain Papa twenty-nine to reach the target. With his pod so close to the alien ship, he didn't dare make a wormhole link with the strike force. Once they were secure, a burst signal would be sent out, a brief energy spike that was common within nebulae. It would appear innocent enough to the Qwin, but would be the signal for Papa to break off his attack.

The pods moved closer, slowly…but not slowly enough.

The cluster struck the metal of the hull with a long shudder that reverberated through Zac's capsule. It had to echo through the aft section of the alien craft as well.

"Hurry, lock us down," he commanded through the short-wave comm of the pods.

"I'm doing the best I can," said Kyle's frustrated voice.

"*Sir.* I'm doing the best I can, *sir*," Zac corrected.

"Permission to say, 'fuck you,' sir."

"Permission denied."

The friendly banter relaxed the REV enough for him to engage the magnetics, and the sustained vibration faded away. The pods were locked down, turned with their backside out, and the darkened viewports facing towards the hull and the other cylinders that made up the nullifying unit. But Zac's pod was at an angle to the rest of the cylinders, meaning the entire string of pods would be the same.

"We're out of alignment," he said into the comm.

"Couldn't help it," said Kyle Johnson. "Let's just hope no one's paying too close attention."

"Roger that," Zac said. He keyed the burst signal.

Victory…of sorts!

The aliens may be gone, but they haven't left. They still occupy over a dozen worlds, many very close to the Solar System. But already we're receiving requests for help from these worlds, help in freeing the inhabitants from the tyranny of the Antaere. You can help. Any donation you can afford will help us in our efforts to save intelligent creatures like us. We're a community now. A community among the stars!

- Fund raising email, Alien Relief Society, 2081.

22

First Insir Bahsor surveyed the battle stats on the screen at his command station. The Humans had only lost two ships to their fire, although nine were out of the battle due to damage. His own force had suffered three complete losses and two damaged. By all rights, the engagement was favored to the Antaere. But his mission was not to engage the enemy, but to provide transport of the Rowin to Iz'zar. He evaluated the fight in those terms.

To continue with the diminished escort all the way to the planet would be a risk, as would returning to Antara. Yet the risk would lessen the closer they got to their homeworld. And the battle was continuing. He could not predict the final outcome, even if it were a victory for the Antaere.

He keyed the comm for the Rowin's vessel.

By the time the slender, yellow-skin royal came on the screen, First Insir Bahsor had made his decision.

"My Lord, I recommend a return to Antara," he said to the young heir-apparent.

Andus Zaphin considered the words for a moment. "Is the battle going against us? I was not aware."

"That is not the reason for my recommendation. There is still a dangerous section of the Grid to cross. Your escort has been diminished. Your safety could be in jeopardy."

The royal sighed, appearing resigned to the outcome. "I had so hoped for a return to the Temple. The spirit there is so much more vibrant than the ancient Temple of Order on Antara." He smiled at the military officer. "Do not tell my father I said that."

Bahsor remained silent.

"Insir, a development," said a voice to Bahsor's right.

He turned to the sound, upset that a crew member would interrupt his conversation with the Rowin.

"The Humans are retreating."

Bahsor returned his attention to Andus. "Pardon me, my Lord."

"Please, I would be interested in the report myself."

"Continue." Bahsor called out to the reporting crew member. "The Humans have retreated before, as a reprieve before resuming their attack."

"Insir, they are engaging gravity drives at a distance and leaving the area."

Bahsor went to the contact screen for confirmation. "My Lord, the Humans are leaving, yet my recommendation still stands."

Andus smiled. "Your sage advice is noted, yet I believe we shall continue to Iz'zar. We must trust in the Order to protect us. Please proceed."

First Insir Bahsor nodded. "Of course, my Lord. Immediately."

Even as the commander began to bark orders for a resumption of the transit to the Temple world, he wished he had the Rowin's confidence in the Order. Sometimes it took more than faith for events to unfold as desired. Sometimes it took caution.

NOTES

Well now they've done it! They've opened a training facility for REVs. Sorry, but bullshit. You can't rain REVs, not the REVs we have today. All you can do is activate them and then get out of the way. That's not very efficient. David doesn't appear very upset. He just made major and strutting around here like a peacock. He's the military's go-to guy now when it comes to NT-4. Frankly, he can have it.

- Journal Entry, July 21, 2079, Dr. Clifford Slater

23

The Twilight was administered to Zac and his four REVs after a return burst signal was received confirming that the mission was a go. The pods were powered down to bare minimal life support. It would take five days to reach Iz'zar, but to the team it would be just a heartbeat. One did not dream while under the influence of Twilight.

They were set to awake as the royal starship was on final approach to the Temple spaceport. Zac snapped out of the prolonged sleep with his mind alert and fresh, although his joints seemed a little stiff and cranky. A few stretches in the confined space of the pod and he was ready to go.

He triggered a tiny camera embedded within the back side of the pod, allowing for a view of the approach to the planet. The other members of the team were doing the same, trying to gain any insight as to the layout of the complex and the surrounding topography. Although they had ample photographic intel, it was always good to get a personal feel for the site.

The huge ship was dropping toward the surface, being

lowered by a small, slowly decaying gravity well seventeen hundred miles above it in the cold of space. At about two thousand feet, the well would fade completely and the huge ship would ride plumes of landing exhaust for the rest of the way down.

Zac panned the camera around. The aft end of the starship was pointed to the south and the shores of a vast ocean about a hundred miles away. There was a contiguous city running from the water all the way to within about ten miles from the walls of the Temple Complex. Beyond a mile-wide buffer, another city formed that continued to the tall, white walls of the Complex. This was where the quarter-million loyal natives lived who were deemed worthy enough to be this close to the revered aliens. According to intel, they were also the first line of defense against a surface attack. The fact that the settlement surrounding the complex resembled a rundown ghetto on Earth made Zac wonder about the effectiveness of such a defensive force. Yet as the ship dropped lower, he noticed how there were no main thoroughfares in the ghetto, just a confused mass of buildings with no defined urban plan. Moving a force up to the gates of the Temple through that would have been impossible. Maybe that was the plan all along.

Zac's view was obscured by roiling clouds of white and gray smoke as the ship neared the surface. That was too bad. They were now within the walls of the complex, and it would have been nice to see more before they touched down.

"Get ready," Zac said through the comm. "Once things settle down outside, the crew will be out inspecting the ship and preparing it for the return trip. The nullifiers are pretty high up and will probably be one of the last things inspected. We should have about an hour to get the document before the pods are discovered."

"Is that when we get to start blowing things up?" Mike asked.

"We'll see. Let's go. There's still a lot of smoke in the area. That will help."

Zac slipped on the full-head mask and then released a side panel in the pod. He slid out, dangling from the edge of the opening to keep from falling to the ground. It was about a hundred feet down. He let go.

Even before landing, Zac felt a slight cascading of strength and energy as his body reacted to the fall. Powerful leg muscles absorbed the force without a problem. The other REVs were plopping to the ground all around him.

They looked up as the sixth pod deposited their backpacks. They caught the packages and immediately locked them into place. They fit on the back of each REV, with two sets of straps that fastened across their waists and chests. The bottom half of the packs were designed to swivel to the front when needed, allowing access to their knocked down rifles and the HK-14 handguns, along with the ammo. The top half carried the uniforms and light sections of armor, should that become necessary.

With whiffs of sweet-smelling exhaust smoke still lingering the air, Zac and his team—dressed in their gaudy mechanics' outfits—marched off toward the main Temple building half a mile away.

The huge complex was made up of several buildings, but the one that stood out the most was the actual Temple of Light. It was a towering dome a hundred stories tall and capped off with a lens two hundred feet in diameter that allowed the light of the yellow sun to enter the vast chamber below. Intricate baffles on the underside of the lens guided the light, directing multiple beams to five-hundred-foot-tall stacks of more crystal lenses, climbing from wide bases until ending at needle-like points halfway toward the arching ceiling. The effect was to cast spectrums of dancing colors along the inner wall, which was coated in mirrors of metal.

The volume of the chamber was immense and designed for the *wow-factor*.

On the floor was a large seating area capable of holding two thousand worshippers, all set before a series of stair-step platforms leading up to a silver-lined podium where the main priest would speak. The seating was reserved for the Antaere exclusively. The native worshippers were herded through side doors and allowed to stand behind barricades along a hundred-eighty-degree arc around the seating area. During sermons, the non-Antaere were kept moving, albeit slowly, so as many followers as possible could pass through the chamber. It wasn't important that they hear the complete sermon just that they attended, for however brief a time.

There were dozens of anterooms, offices and other areas along the outer perimeter of the sermon room designed to serve the faithful. And the entire interior of the Temple was kept spotless, with only reverent tones spoken while on the floor.

Besides the sheer grandeur the spectacle of the chamber, there was also a balance and order, the prime directives of the Antaere race. Although overwhelming to the average citizen, everything inside the Temple was to scale without appearing outsized or grandiose. There was beauty and function, meaning and respect.

During their tenure, the Antaere had built a smaller version of the Temple on Earth, so the Humans had a pretty good idea as to the layout of the building. Underneath the main structure was where the business took place, including church administration, the priests' quarters...and their study library. The Temple on Earth contained only a few rare volumes of Antaere teachings, and none of the Corollaries. There was a stripped-down version of the Book of Order—every Temple had one—but none of the one-or-two of a kind of documents you find on either Antara or Iz'zar. And where the temple of Earth had nine lower levels, the Temple of Light had twelve.

On Earth the library was on the lowest level, so mission planners assumed that would be where Zac and his REVs would find the one on Iz'zar.

The grounds surrounding the Temple were what gave the complex its impression of size. It was four miles across and formed into an octagon, with the spaceport to the rear, the Temple in the center and security barracks running along the walls to the left and right. In the vast courtyard to the front of the Temple dome were two sets of ornamental buildings along a ceremonial path from the main gate to the front of the Temple. In the distant past, this tiled walkway had been used for grand parades by Antaere royalty and other dignitaries. Yet with the squalor now outside the walls, no one entered through the main gates anymore. Inside they arrived by starship or shuttle, or through the cleaner gates near the troop quarters. The natives—when they were allowed to attend the services—were brought through an entrance along the south wall, paraded through the sermon chamber, and then spit out through another gate to the north.

As Zac and his men walked toward the massive dome, he checked the gate to the north. It was visible from the tarmac of the spaceport and appeared to be lightly guarded. There was no sermons scheduled, at least not that the natives could attend. With the arrival of the Rowin, the Temple grounds had been cleared of any outsiders, and now only Antaere occupied the vast complex.

There was a grand entrance along the side of the Temple facing the spaceport. Guards, dressed in ceremonial attire, were stationed there and eyed the five approaching workers with distain.

One of the Qwin with a bright yellow collar on his blue coat was shaking his head. "Restricted, you know this. What are you doing off the ship?"

Zac reached around and tapped his hard-shelled backpack. "Special coding equipment for the Rowin," he said through the translator bug he had implanted behind his right ear. It would take his Human speak and seamlessly convert it to Antaere. The movement of his lips would be out of sync with the words spoken, but the full-face mask hid his mouth from the guards.

"Be that so, you must still use the service entrance on the side."

"Forgive us, first visit to the Temple."

He led his men around the side, still feeling the lead guard's eyes on his back until they turned the corner. There were more guards at the next entrance, but after another set of questions, they were allowed inside.

The service entrance didn't open directly into the Grand Chamber, but rather a utilitarian lobby area that branched off into corridors leading either along the side of the building or to stairways and elevators to access the lower levels.

And there were Qwin everywhere, all conveying a buzz of energy in anticipation of the Rowin entering the building. Unlike Zac and his REVs, the royal would enter through the main entrance and into the Grand Chamber. There were accommodations for the royal family under the main sermon level, although he wouldn't spend much time there. The royalty of the Antaere spent a lot of time among the commoners of their race. They said it was to bind them to the masses, when in fact it was merely an ego thing for the bloodline. Honor and acceptance of their position was expected; it was part of the Order of the Universe. For people to do otherwise was almost incomprehensible, especially among the Antaere. Yet as the race reached into space and encountered other species, they didn't always get the respect they deserved. They were cruel and vindictive when this happened on worlds without advanced technology or a formidable military. For those that did, the Antaere were more subtle with their revenge.

Earth had been one of those worlds, where billions refused to bow down to the glory of the aliens. Of course there were a few who did, and they helped initiate the war with the Qwin through their terrorist activities against their own race. Humans can be threatened and intimidated into obeying for only so long. After that, all bets were off.

But on Iz'zar, the minority of non-believers lived a more cautious and clandestine existence. There were plenty of them for sure, but they didn't show themselves to others or make huge demonstrations against the Antaere. That would have been fatal.

The aliens had been on the planet for two hundred years and for most of that time, the Antaere were the only star-traveling species with the technology to subjugate entire planets. Then the Humans got involved. Now with a second star-traveling race—and one with military skills that rivaled the Qwin—resistance to the Order was spreading across all the advanced worlds of the Grid. Although Iz'zar was immune to the more violent uprisings, there was still a sizeable network of non-believers that Zac and his team would use to make their escape from the planet, if they got that far.

The team began to make their way down into the depths of the Antaere Temple. The first two levels—out of twelve—proved a non-issue. No one gave them a second glance as they were too busy preparing for the Rowin's arrival to pay attention to anything but their own tasks. Yet the lower they went, the tighter the security. The High Priests lived down here, with the last six levels dedicated to them exclusively. There were cafeterias, residences, meeting rooms; even grooming stations of questionable repute.

Eventually the team came to an immoveable force…in the form of a defiant Antaere female.

"You will not pass. I am surprised you are here at this level. You should not have been allowed."

"How then are we to deliver these filters to the Enlightenment Chamber? Without them the sacred text could become damaged."

"I have no record of such a maintenance request. And what are these uniforms you wear? I have never seen such. They appear to serve no purpose…other than to hide your appearance." The expression on the alien's face changed….

Zac had no choice. He stepped around the counter to where the female was standing and took a swipe at her. He'd learned his lesson back at Camp Slater not to hit as hard as he was able. He didn't want to kill the female, just knock her out a little.

But if one had never hit someone with the purpose of only rendering them unconscious, one would have a tendency not to give it their all. And Zac did just that. He didn't knock her out; all he did was make her mad.

Antaere females are every bit a match for the males, sometimes even stronger, if not definitely meaner. The Qwin recovered from the hit instantly and jumped with spongy legs onto Zac's chest, wrapping strong legs around his torso and her arms around his head. She ripped off his mask and begin to bite at his neck.

The other REVs were on her in a second, easily pulling her off their leader. Donovan wasn't so subtle, and a moment later the Qwin female was laid out on the floor, dead.

Zac's mask was in shreds, which took away his disguise, not only for the remainder of the mission to the Enlightenment Chamber, but also on the way out.

"Feisty little bitch, wasn't she," Mike said.

"Get her behind the counter in case someone comes along," Zac ordered. "You guys are going to have to give me cover from here on." They were on the eighth level, with four to go. And that was assuming the Enlightenment Chamber was at the lowest level.

They were in a huge room with a ceiling twice as high as the other floors. This was definitely VIP territory. But the place was empty; a condition Zac credited to the arrival of the Rowin. Either the priests were already in position to greet him, or they were in their chambers getting ready.

They moved across the room to a bank of lifting platforms. The other floors had traditional elevators, but down here there were a series of rotating platforms, like a circular escalator. With this setup, no priest would have to wait for an elevator. It essentially put all the floors on the same level.

Just as the team was about to step on, a group of six elaborately adorned Antaere swung up on the back platform to face them. There was a moment of uncertainty, as the aliens sized up the four uniformed figures—and one Human. They recognized Zac instantly; Humans were the greatest threat the Antaere had ever faced. Everyone knew what they looked like.

Zac rushed forward, slamming two of the priests toward the back of the platform. They fell back and onto the next one, with Zac on top. He was surprised at the viciousness with which they fought—until he remembered he'd never fought a Qwin outside of a Run. He had no idea how they fought as a general rule. After the female—and now the priests—he was beginning to understand why they were such a tough enemy. They fought like wild dogs.

However, the six aliens were no match for the REVs. Without holding back, it took just one hit each to crush their skulls. But now all hell broke loose. The bodies had continued to ride the rotating escalator where other priests and assistants could see them. There was panic, with calls being made to security. Other Qwin, curious about the commotion, were coming out of their rooms on the eighth level. Seeing the carnage, they either raced forward to attack the Humans, or ducked back inside to make more calls.

"Looks like the need for stealth is over," Angus yelled above the screeching of *qwin, qwin, qwin*. He pulled off his head mask before pressing a button on the side of his backpack. The lower section spun around on a built-in rail. He had the M-101 out, extended and slung around his shoulder two seconds later. The HK-14 came next, with extra magazines held in pockets on the rifle's strap. He stuck the handgun in a pocket of his Qwin uniform. A flick of a release, and the backpack section fell away.

He took the M-101 in his hands, sighted a group of Qwin emerging from one of the side rooms, and fired. He wasn't the only one. By now all five REVs were locked and loaded. The room was cleared of enemy three seconds later.

They stepped onto the escalator and rotated down to the next level. Qwin were here, too, but most were running for their lives. Zac smiled. Now this was more like he was used to. He fired at the retreating aliens.

Then he stopped. No matter how much he enjoyed killing aliens, the team couldn't spend too much time at it. They had to get to the Enlightenment Chamber before the Corollaries were destroyed.

"Let's go!" he yelled to his team, who were literally giddy as they shot the aliens.

They followed him through the spinning platforms, hopping from one to the other to go deeper under the Temple. They reached the bottom-most level and discovered it was of a different design from the others, definitely less traveled with ornately decorated walls of wood relief, plush carpeting and a heavy wooden door at the center on a long, wide corridor.

Zac raced up to the door while two of the REVs covered the escalator and the other two each side of the corridor. There was a thick, black iron handle on the door, and when he pulled, it opened. Zac was as shocked as anyone that it wasn't locked. But when he stepped through the entrance his spirits fell. This was just the showcase entrance. The rear entrance was inside the anteroom.

This was a set of shiny metal doors, devoid of handles, with only an electronic key pad for entry. On either side of the portal were wide windows looking into a well-lit room with high ceilings. There were rows of low bookshelves, tables and ancient-looking books sealed in containers resting atop elaborate podiums. This was definitely the Enlightenment Chamber. The half dozen Antaere huddled over bound texts was the other giveaway. Those inside the room spotted the Humans and began to move.

Zac stepped back and fired a burst from his rifle at one of the windows. The glass spider-webbed but didn't break. He tried again, with the same result. It was worth a try. He turned his attention to the door, and all a blast at the control pad did was knock it off the door, leaving a mass of sparking wires.

Out of frustration, he slammed the stock of his weapon on the metal door. If he was activated, he would simply batter the doors down with his body. As it was, he now had to *think* of a solution. Sometimes that wasn't as easy as it sounds.

The Qwin inside the Enlightenment Chamber were talking on communicators, reporting the intruders. Anytime now someone in the building would figure out why they were there and order the destruction of the Final Glory document. That's when Zac noticed a couple of the Qwin disappear around a wall to the right. From what he could see of the room, there shouldn't be more than ten feet behind the wall before it met with the outer wall to the corridor.

His throat mic was active. "Angus, Kyle, check to the right. See if there's another entrance."

Zac heard a pair of quick rifle bursts in that direction.

"Roger that, LT. Caught two of them coming out. They left it open for us with their bodies."

More gunfire, this time from the left.

"Report," Zac called out.

"We've got company!' said Donovan Ross.

"How many?"

"Well, about all of them. They're on the escalators, but just found an express elevator of some kind. They're pouring out of there, too."

"Kyle, Angus, support Mike and Don. I'll go in the room alone. Hold them back until I find the document."

He raced past Kyle and Angus as they headed in the other direction toward the escalator. Stepping over the bodies of the two dead Qwin priests, he entered the side door to the Enlightenment Chamber.

This entrance was simple, with barely a deadbolt. It seemed even the heavy interior security door was more for show. Day-to-day access to the room was through the side door.

Zac blasted a couple of running Qwin when he reached the

main chamber. He couldn't risk any true believers making their last great sacrifice by destroying the Final Glory text. He looked around. "If I were a set of Corollaries, where would I be," he said aloud. They would be special, revered, so possibly in one of the sealed cases.

He moved to the nearest podium. There was a huge book resting on an ornate stand, with a black leather cover etched in silver ink. He shrugged the upper half of his backpack off his shoulders and opened it. There was an optical reader inside. He took the unit, and through the glass cover, ran the broad end over the book. The screen on the top device displayed the translated the text.

Order of the Universe....

There was more text, and although this book was something special, it wasn't what they'd come for.

He raced to three other podiums, aware that there was a firefight taking place in the outside corridor and that he didn't have a lot of time.

He spotted a Qwin—a young one—hiding behind a bookcase. He ran to the alien and pointed the M-101 at his head. "The Corollaries...where are they!"

The alien trembled, as his eyes shifted unconsciously to the right. He was too afraid to speak, but he didn't have to. Zac moved to the pedestal.

Under the glass was a thin set of square pages, fanned out like playing cards. There was a small heading on each page and then blocks of writing. Zac ran his reader along the pages.

Corollaries of Order.

He lifted his rifle and slammed the stock into the protective cover. It shattered, showering the ancient documents in shards of glass. He brushed away the debris and scooped up all the documents. He took them to a table and did a quick scan. There! *Final*

Glory of Mentar, Universal Corollaries to the Order of Light. This had to be it.

Zac took the full sheet—it was only a single sheet—and slipped it under the tight-fitting top of his Antaere uniform. It would be safe there—unless he was shot in the chest. He headed out the way he came.

"I got it," he reported over the comm.

"Just in time; I'm low on ammo," Mike reported.

"Me too," said Angus.

"Time to kick some alien ass!" Donovan cried out. "Rock on REVs!"

NOTES

The New REV doll every red-blooded boy needs this Holiday Season. Simple to use and all action. Just wind him up…and let him go!

- Facebook ad, December 2, 2086

24

The Antaere troops had thinned out by now, either dead or retreated to a stronger position. Zac's REVs were pressed into doorways, covering the rotating escalator and the open doorway of the elevator. The elevator was something special, with its existence hidden within the wall reliefs, either on purpose or not to disturb the reverent feel to the hallway. It was a way to gain access to the Enlightenment Chamber without having to cycle through each floor. It would have been nice to know that ahead of time, Zac thought. It would have saved a lot of time…and ammunition.

During the lull in the battle, the REVs were taking turns changing out of their gaudy starship engineer suit and into their uniforms. If they were to die, they wanted to die looking good. Besides the fatigues, they attached shoulder and chest armor onto fastening anchors. These were thin pieces of composite material, lightweight but extremely tough. The chest plate had the distinctive raised sword of the REVs with a red stripe running away to each side and up toward the shoulder pads. They strapped utility belts around their waists and placed the HK-14s into the attached holsters. As one REV would dress, the others covered him. Three minutes and the team had the look of a squad of killer REVs ready for action.

"The elevator," Zac called out. "Cover me."

The team opened up on the escalator, driving away any lurking aliens. Zac sprinted to the open doorway and kicked away several dead Qwin, even as he scooped up four of their weapons and tossed them inside the cab. He surveyed the carriage before jumping up and grasping an overhead panel. With his REV strength, he yanked down, tearing the metal sheet away. He continued to rip at the ceiling until the top of the elevator was open to the dark shaft above it.

The elevator ran by magnetics, not cables, but that didn't matter. Here was a way out, and without all the accompanying obstacles they would encounter taking the traditional route. He signaled for his men, one at a time, to race past the escalator and to the elevator, while the others provided cover. Even if the Qwin wanted to time their shots to the crossing, the REVs moved in a blur, taking a blink of an eye to cover the distance. Even before everyone was across, others had taken up the extra weapons and were climbing into the elevator shaft.

There were struts and supports all the way up which where like a jungle gym to the Humans. With extraordinary strength and coordination, the men literally flung themselves upward, gaining a level every couple of seconds.

"Looks like a control unit up above," Donovan reported. He was in the lead and would reach the top of the shaft first. "This could be our exit."

Just then, rifle slugs began to ricochet off the walls of the elevator shaft, being fired from below. Kyle took a round in his left thigh and lost his footing, falling away into the center of the shaft. He dropped a full level before Zac reached out and grabbed him around the neck. Kyle gasped, unable to breathe until he was pressed against a cross beam along the wall and wrapped his arms around the metal strut.

"Crude, but effective," he coughed. "Thanks."

Zac was already scrambling upward and didn't reply.

Dodging incoming fire from below, the team reached the top of the shaft. There was a closed door, which Zac figured would open to a firing squad of Qwin, having been alerted by those below. He looked up and spotted a narrow gap between the elevator's control unit and the wall of the shaft. He sent his men squeezing through until they were all standing on top of the metal control box.

There was an access panel on the wall, used by maintenance personnel for the elevator. Zac kicked it and the panel fell away… and down onto the waiting Qwin.

The panel didn't hurt any of the aliens; it just startled them. But by the time they reacted, Zac's REVs were flinging themselves through the opening and tumbling to the floor outside the elevator, weapons firing non-stop.

The Antaere who weren't cut down by the metal slugs were crushed by powered blows from the Humans. The fight lasted only seconds before Zac had his people sprinting across the wide service corridor they'd left almost half an hour before. But now the place was a madhouse, filled with confused and panicking aliens, intermixed with an influx of armored troops rushing in from outside.

Zac rushed to a service counter made of stone and ripped off the top. He tossed it down the tiled corridor. It slid, cutting the feet out from under a dozen troops, while others tried to jump the speeding object. Distracted, they became easy targets for the REVs, who in a state of cascading were finding their target acquisition abilities improving by the second. The fire was so rapid that it sounded like one continuous shot. Qwin died by the dozen, as the team would empty one weapon only to scoop up another and keep firing, with only a heartbeat's delay.

"We can't keep this up," Zac said from behind a counter, as slugs shattered everything around him. "There are a lot more them than there are of us. We have to get outside."

"I have several doorways over here," Mike reported from his position. "They're along the outer wall; could be another way out other than the way we came."

"Angus, go with him. We'll provide cover."

The two REVs crashed through the first door, using their bodies rather than the handle. Flashes from their weapons lasted a second before the all-clear was given.

"Just a room, but more doors. Completing our sweep."

Zac ducked a barrage of bullets as they ripped at the wall above him "Hurry up. It's getting dicey here."

"Bingo!" said Angus over the comm. "Not a door, but a panel of windows looking out. A whole boatload of Qwin are running past, heading for the service entrance. You're going to have even more company in about two seconds."

"We're on our way."

The rest of the team ran into the first room and then the second. Angus and Mike hadn't broken through the window yet, not until they were all there. When the last of the advancing aliens had run pass the window, Mike took the stock of a Qwin weapon to the glass. This wasn't any special bullet-proof material and it broke away easily. He cleared a section and hopped through to the outside.

He was spotted immediately, which was unfortunate for the Qwin who turned their weapons on him. He was much quicker.

On this side of the Temple dome was a cluster of small buildings, as well as the North Gate and the beginning of the half-mile-long barracks for the security troops that ran along the interior of the border wall. Even with the main contingent of security units having moved into the dome, there were still plenty of loose Qwin around to fire on them. Besides that, the main force was being alerted to their position. Qwin were appearing everywhere.

Zac led his men through a barrage a fire and straight into the advancing Qwin. Friendly fire began to cut into the aliens, even as all the REVs took hits of one degree or the other. Fortunately, there were so many bodies rushing about that the Humans became lost in the mad crush. They slipped behind one of the outbuildings and took inventory.

"How bad are you hurt?" Zac asked the team. Each sounded off. Mike appeared to be the worst off, with three wounds, including one to his lower abdomen. He was bleeding badly. Zac had two wounds himself, both in his legs. He felt the pain, but it was numbed to a degree by the cascading taking place in his body. The natural NT-4 was doing its job.

He glanced to the east and the small spaceport within the Temple grounds. There was a lingering cloud of smoke, left over from when the Rowin's ship was evacuated from the surface at the outset of the battle. It was a natural reaction. But now a multitude of small atmospheric fighter planes were either landing or taking off. Soon the sky would be filled with them, all looking for Zac and his team. It was bad enough facing the ground troops. Threats from the sky would be the last straw.

Behind them was the north wall—rising forty feet up—with the well-guarded gate five hundred feet to the west. The wall was wide enough for guards to patrol the top. Most had clustered near the gate, expecting the Humans to try to break out there.

Zac sized up the leap it would take for them to reach the top of the wall. Forty feet in Earth-normal gravity, that was asking a lot. He had an idea.

"One of us will catapult the rest to the top. Then we'll hang one down by his wrists while the man on the ground makes a leap for his legs. He'll then climb over the other to the top. It should work."

"I'll take the bottom," Mike volunteered.

They rushed to the wall. Angus was the first up. With a boost from Mike, he reached the top with his fingertips. He lifted himself up and rolled over onto the top of the wall. Zac went next, grabbing Angus's outstretched hand. He was up and in covering position a second later. Guards on the wall near the gate noticed the Humans and came running. Without any cover, Zac cut them down with three center mass shots from two hundred feet away.

Donovan came next, followed by Kyle, who with Angus holding his wrists, dangled along the inner side of the wall.

"C'mon Mike!" Donovan called out.

Mike stood back, looked up at the wall, and then to the spaceport half a mile away.

"Mike! Hurry."

"You guys go on without me. I'm bleeding like a sieve; I won't last much longer."

"Bullshit!"

Zac heard the conversation. "Sergeant, get your ass up here. That's an order."

"Sorry, Zac." Mike called up. "I'll provide air cover. Get out of here. It's all right."

Zac looked down at the man, who was grimacing and

holding his side. "Do you even know how to fly one of those things?"

"I'm a fast learner. Now go, LT. Go."

More Qwin were climbing to the top of the wall, coming from both sides now, as the small aircraft lifted off and gained altitude, looking for a target. They were sitting ducks on the wall.

"Good luck, Mike."

Mike Brickey ran off along the wall, still clutching his side but faster than any of the aliens trying to catch him.

Zac couldn't wait any longer. On the other side of the wall was a fifty foot buffer where the Antaere didn't allow any native buildings. Beyond that, however, was the ugly sprawl of a shantytown. With Zac remaining on the wall for cover, the remaining three REVs jumped to the ground, their REV-enhanced leg muscles absorbing the shock of the landing. They sprinted off to the cover of the slum buildings. Zac followed a few seconds later, just as enemy slugs tore into the part of the wall he'd just left.

The team didn't linger. They ran into the urban sprawl, zig-zagging between huts and lean-tos, avoiding the few natives they found along the way. It seemed that when the call went out to defend the Temple most had made their way to the main entrance, expecting a frontal assault. Few realized the threat was already within the compound. Now the streets were virtually deserted. What natives they did encounter didn't live to tell about it.

Zac had a small locator with him, carried in the backpack until needed. Now he turned it on. It would guide them to the extraction point where they would meet up with the locals who would get them off the planet. He was rewarded with a strong signal, about two miles out and to the east, on the opposite side of the Temple wall from the spaceport.

"Mike, how you doing?" he asked through his comm.

"Just reached the spaceport, about to commandeer a ride. Where are you?" Mike's voice was filled of agony.

"Heading east through the city. Extraction point is just on the other side of the wall from your location. If you get a chance, land your vehicle on this side. We'll try to get you out."

"Don't bother. I have other plans."

NOTES

People around the world continue to mourn the death last Saturday of Doctor Clifford Slater, the prominent scientist credited with taking a once-illicit performance-enhancing drug and turning it into one of the greatest weapons we have against the Antaere threat....

- Obituary, December 30, 2088

25

Mike Brickey ran up to one of the small, one-alien aircraft and pulled the pilot from the cockpit. He jumped inside and closed the canopy.

The plane ran on lifting fans and chemical fuel, with vertical takeoff capabilities. Mike had no idea how to fly it, so he took the control stick and pressed it forward. The craft skidded along the ground, plowing through a group of Qwin who had come to stop him. That was fortunate, but he really needed to get airborne.

There was another control stick on his right. He grabbed it and pressed it forward. The plane lurched, nearly burying its nose into the tarmac before he could stop it. He pulled back on the stick and the plane lifted off.

He relaxed his grip and evened out the stick. The plane leveled out, but it wasn't moving forward. The center stick did the trick. Using a combination of both controls, he lifted higher and began to move forward, in the direction of the north wall.

Other craft were launching and coming after him. Small bursts of plasma energy were erupting from the other planes. He pulled the center control stick over and the plane banked to the left. The barrage of bolts missed him. The second round wouldn't.

Mike had no idea how to fire the weapons or even how to increase speed. There were no foot pedals, so he was at a loss. All he could do was move forward, gain or lose altitude and bank.

He grimaced with pain, with a spasm in his side so severe that he almost passed out. This had to be serious when even the natural NT-4 couldn't dull the pain enough for him to stay conscious. There wasn't much time left. If he couldn't provide air cover for the team….then he needed a diversion.

He glanced out the side of the plane and down on the huge dome below. Staring up at him was the round eye of the crystal lens, aglow in the light of mid-day on Iz'zar. "Why not?" he groaned. "Probably won't do much, but what the hell. It's worth a try."

Taking both controls firmly in his hands, he banked the plane over and accelerated. A moment later he buried the nose into the lens, fully expecting to bounce off the thick crystal. He didn't. Instead, the massive lens shattered.

As the roof crumbled, the sides of the dome began to collapse inward, creating a series of explosive sounds as supports broke and walls crumbled. Layer by layer the one-hundred-story tall building fell, until the debris reached the ground level and smashed deeper into the underground sections. When the downward motion of the falling debris ended, a roiling cloud of white dust shot skyward, channeled by the surviving walls of the dome. Rather than spread out, the cloud billowed up like a fountain, before forming a mushroom top about three thousand feet in the air.

26

Zac and the team were nearly knocked off their feet by the rumbling of the ground. Some of the weaker huts around them collapsed, causing the REVs to dive for cover. When they looked up, they saw the cloud of dust rising up from where the Temple had once stood.

"Did Mike find a nuke somewhere?" Donovan asked.

"That's not nuclear," Kyle corrected. "The dude just took out the whole damn Temple!"

Zac looked around. There were natives around, all gawking at the rising mushroom cloud.

"Move out," Zac ordered. "Let's get to the rendezvous spot while everyone's distracted."

"I'm pretty distracted myself...and in awe," Angus said. "Damn, Mike!"

Five minutes later the four remaining members of the team

reached the location highlighted on the small screen. A native appeared out of a doorway and called them inside. There were six others in the room.

The Kalori—as the natives of Iz'zar were called—were of Human height and build, but with six fingers, four ears and a pair of eyes placed on the end of inch-long stalks. Their skin was leathery, with patterns resembling scales.

"What did you do!" the leader cried out. "You were to only acquire an ancient document. Why have you destroyed the Temple of Light?"

All the Kalori in the room were agitated and nervous. Some looked out windows, while others stared at the Humans, appearing ready to attack. The REVs raised their weapons.

"Everyone stay cool," Zac said. "We have the document."

"And matters so?" asked one of the other natives. "This is beyond!"

Zac didn't want to reveal too many details about their mission, confident that this level of native resistance wasn't privy to the full story. "Don't worry, things will settle out once the contents of the document are revealed. That was the purpose of the mission. The Temple was just collateral damage."

The leader shook his head. "This is far too serious."

Zac stepped closer, his weapon menacingly close to the alien. "Are you going to help us or not?"

"Can you assure liberation through the document? That is all that matters."

Zac nodded. "That's the plan. Now make up your mind. We don't have all day."

"We will help, but only to get you off Iz'zar before you can be traced to us."

"That's all we ask. Lead on."

The team was dressed in over-sized hoods and capes and put aboard a native car. A small caravan of three transports wound its way through the ghetto before emerging on a dirt road heading into the mountains. The trip took longer than Zac anticipated, but they were heading away from the Temple Complex. The cloud still lingered in the sky, turning golden as this fateful day was coming to an end.

About an hour after dark, the caravan pulled up to a small airfield dotted with aircraft of conventional design.

"Where are we?" Zac asked.

The native leader—who refused to give his name for fear of being found out—had not spoken a word for the entire three hours of the trip.

"This is a crop sanitizing center, used to protect against insects and the like."

"I don't see any starships here," Angus pointed out. "How are we supposed to get off the planet?"

"Under the canopy there you will find transport. It is a simple lifting shuttle, old yet functional."

The transports pulled up beside the covered spacecraft. Natives climbed out and pulled the canvas away.

"Do you have a pilot among you?" the unnamed leader of the Kalori asked.

"No we don't."

The alien seemed particularly perturbed. He turned to one of the natives standing nearby, looking angry and defiant.

"I implore you, Nanno," said the leader. "Only get them to the ship, then move to Roswor. That will mask your return."

The younger native turned and entered the rusty-skinned shuttle, mumbling to himself as he did so.

"Are you sure this thing can make it?" Kyle asked.

"It has good function. We of the non-believers use it often. The exterior has been disguised."

The team entered the shuttle. Zac thanked the leader, who just turned and walked away into the darkness.

The shuttle actually worked quite well, and thirty minutes later, the team floated weightless on the bridge as the young native pilot closed in on a bulky, ugly star freighter. Everything having to do with the Kalori seemed old and rundown, causing Zac to wonder if this was what became of species after two hundred years of Antaere rule? Fortunately, humanity had been able to throw off their yoke before it was too late.

The shuttle moved into the freighter's landing bay. An atmosphere was established and the team stepped into sub-freezing temperature as they double-timed it to an airlock. The Kalori shuttle was gone before they knew it, leaving the four Humans standing in a small, unattended room next to the bay's control room.

Zac felt the engines engage. They were going somewhere, but where?

A locking handle on a hatchway moved up, and the door opened. An alien Zac recognized as an Enif stepped over the threshold. The alien had a huge bulge for a forehead, looking like one of those big-brain creatures from the old science fiction videos. Zac knew better. The Enif weren't very smart.

"Leader?" the alien asked.

Zac stepped forward. "Lieutenant Zac Murphy," he said as an introduction. It still felt awkward to call himself *lieutenant*.

"I be Wisn, captain. Follow."

The team obeyed and were taken to the bridge. There were four other alien crew, all Enif except one. He was a Kalori. The Iz'zar native took the lead.

"I am called Finsic. We are heading out system at maximum speed. The Antaere are just now launching forces to track you. We will continue on this course for another hour before reversing course."

"Reversing?"

"Yes. The Antaere are looking for vessels heading out-system. We will appear to be arriving."

"And then what?" Zac asked.

"Then we will return to Iz'zar."

"What...why?"

The alien looked impatient. "You will remain there for several days until the search is called off. Then you will be moved off planet and to a waiting Human starship a light-year from here. It is what has been deemed the safest option."

Zac nodded his approval. Although he didn't like the idea of returning to Iz'zar, the plan made since. He just hoped none of the natives would have second thoughts about helping them. He would hate to have to kill them.

The freighter was challenged by an Antaere ship, but was allowed to proceed when told they were heading for the planet rather than away. After clearing that hurdle, Zac and his men were shown to a small work area off the landing bay, with a couple of tables and chairs enough for the four of them. They spent a few minutes in quiet reverence for their fallen comrade.

"Well, that didn't turn out exactly as planned," said Angus, breaking the silence. "We better hope that document is enough to cover our arses."

"What does it say, Zac…I mean lieutenant." Kyle wasn't being funny, just accurate.

Zac was curious about the document, too. He removed the ancient Antaere script from the protective plastic pouch it was in. The translation device was in a pocket of his fatigues. He laid the square page on a table and began to scan the text.

"Final Glory of Mentar, Universal Corollaries to the Order of Light," he recited.

"That sounds like what we were looking for," Kyle remarked.

The reader scanned each line and then made the translation. Zac continued.

"In the glory of the Universal Light, we issue these Corollaries for guidance and wisdom to the Order. Shall they be followed in their entirety.

"The Glory of the Antaere shall be Final as Order spreads across the Universe, achieved through the light of the yellow stars which give birth to the followers of the Order. Until such time as Order is achieved, the Guardians shall use the labors of the followers to assist in bringing Order to the Universe. Upon the time of the Final Glory, the Guardians are to initiate processes regarding the followers as prescribed here."

"Here it comes," Zac said as he moved the reader to the next line of text.

"Upon the Final Glory, when Order comes to the Universe, all followers of the Light shall be welcomed into the Glory, to share with the Antaere eternal peace and joy in the Order. Until that time, the Guardians will encourage and assist the followers to achieve the greatest Glory in their own lives and on their own worlds. We are one. We shall be one at the Final Glory."

Zac stopped scanning, picked up the sheet and turned it over. There was nothing on the back. That was it.

"Holy crap—literally," Kyle said. "That's not what we were told it would say."

Zac was stunned, on a variety of levels. First: As Kyle said, this is not what the document was supposed to say. Not even close. And second: There was nothing here that would shield them—and Earth—from what just took place on Iz'zar.

"We're in some deep shit," Donovan said. "And I mean all of us. We can't release that text. If we do, all it will do is strengthen the Antaere hold on their followers, not lessen it."

Zac stared at the ancient, yellowed document. Maybe things had changed since it had been written. Maybe the new strategy of the Antaere was as they'd been told. But where was the proof? Where was the document that would vindicate the Humans for what they'd just done? The sheet of paper on the table in front of him wasn't it.

Zac could see the shitstorm forming that General Smith has spoken of a month before. This wasn't good, not at all.

27

It took the team three weeks to make it back to Camp Slater. Along the way, they monitored Grid-wide broadcasts, and the near-endless looping of stories about the destruction of the Temple of Light. And it didn't take long for the Antaere to identify who did it.

They were now broadcasting videos showing close ups of Zac and his team mowing down unarmed and elaborately-dressed priests in cold blood…and laughing as they did. Zac had to admit; they did do a fair amount of laughing, but that was just a reaction to being back in the REV saddle again, and not out of any morbid delight in the killing. But no one was speaking up for them. In fact, there was a news blackout coming out of Earth. They had no comment on the Temple fiasco.

Now, as Zac made his way to the admin building for a meeting with General Smith, he could see the storm cloud gathering, and he was right in their path.

"What went wrong, lieutenant?" Smith asked as Zac took a seat. The tone of his voice wasn't accusatory, but more rhetorical.

"The intel was faulty, general. That means we were set up."

"That may be so, but we have no way of proving it."

The general shook his head and opened a file on this desk, not to read it, but out of habit. "Did you really have to destroy the Temple?" he asked. "I told you what would happen if you did."

"Would you believe it if I said it was an accident?"

"A hundred story dome structure, built like a brick shithouse…and the five you took it down—by accident."

"Actually, that was Sergeant Brickey."

Smith knew the details already. He just needed to vent.

"So how bad is it?" Zac asked.

"Worse than we could have imagined," the general began. "Every ES world where we've had operations have now pulled their support. Even on planets we've secured we're being asked to leave, and any resistance that may have been on those worlds has either dissolved or gone deep underground. There are even calls for a unified force to be sent against Earth. That's not gaining much support, but the Antaere seem to be toying with the idea, seeing that they now have almost unanimous support in the Grid."

"That wouldn't be advised."

"You would think not," said General Smith. "But the small faction of Sun worshippers on Earth are back at it again, accusing their own kind of the most heinous atrocities, real and imagined. This is only one of hundreds of deadly events or accidents being blamed on the Humans. If an alien breaks a fingernail, it's our fault. And this is just the beginning."

Zac was hesitant to broach the subject, but he had to. "What about us? I've seen the videos. They make us out to be a bunch of blood-thirsty killers. REVs already had a pretty nasty reputation in the Grid. This isn't helping."

Smith averted his eyes, looking down at his desk and shuffling some papers. When he looked back at Zac, his eyes were filled with worry. "There's talk back of Earth of throwing you guys under the bus, to make it out as a rogue operation by a bunch of former REVs all strung out on a new version of the drug."

Zac saw this coming. He nodded. "Makes sense," he said. "Even I might believe it. You're not going to let them do that, are you, general?"

"It may be out of my hands, son," said the general. "But there is plenty of evidence showing this was a sanctioned operation."

"If the evidence stays intact."

The general nodded. "Until then, I'm sending all of you to a new facility Colonel Cross has set up. It's back on Earth, so you'll be protected from any aliens out for vengeance."

"What about my fellow man?" Zac asked sarcastically. "You know they'd stab us in the back if there was even the slightest chance of gaining favor with the rest of the Grid."

"You'll go in secret; no one but Cross and his staff will know you're there."

"I don't trust that guy,' Zac said. "He's not what he seems to be."

"Right now he's about the only friend you have."

Zac sensed the meeting was over. He rose to his feet, shook the general's hand and then left the office. He had packing to do.

28

Andus Zaphin was the Rowin of the Antaere, the next in line to lead the Guardians of Order and all the worshippers of the yellow stars. He was the second of his father's male offspring, yet personally selected to be Rowin. He had more intelligence and sense than his siblings, and his father knew it. That was fortunate. He would have regretted having to kill his older brother. They were good friends.

Now Andus walked among the rubble of the Temple of Light on Iz'zar, accompanied by his loyal counselor and friend, Congin Bornak. It had been thirty days since its destruction, and still very little cleanup had begun. That was by design.

Andus bent down and picked up a large clump of crystal, part of the huge lens that had once capped the dome. Andus had spent many a day within the Grand Chamber, either listening to Order sermons or conducting them himself. He had felt the light on his skin through the massive lens. It gave him strength and wisdom.

But now it was gone, along with the entire Temple.

"There is pressure to begin the reconstruction, my Lord," said Congin. "I have delayed the requests, as per your instructions."

"Good. We must leave the ruins as they are for longer, much longer. Each day the ruins remain, our support grows stronger."

"As was the plan."

Andus dropped the crystal to the ashes covering the ground. "It was regrettable that we had to allow the Temple to be destroyed. I did so enjoy being here."

"It was necessary, my Lord. And you must be pleased that your plan progressed even better than initially formulated."

"That is true, thanks to the reckless aggression of the Human savages." Andus laughed. "And they believed they had achieved so much by reaching the Enlightenment Chamber, when in fact it was all we could do to give them safe passage. It must have been disheartening when they read the Corollary and its false message. It has left them with no avenue from which to escape the ridicule. However, it was when the Human crashed the air vehicle into the dome, that their final humiliation was achieved. Even then, the explosives hidden within the Temple made for a dramatic spectacle. I commend your recommendation for such, Congin."

"I was soon to trigger the devices if the battle continued much longer, until the opportunity arose."

"You did well," said Andus. "But now it is time to move on and complete the plan as originally set out. We must eliminate the Human threat from the Grid. And with this single event, resistance to the Order has vanished. Our worlds have been returned to us after the temporary interference from Earth and their non-believers. We are free to do as we wish, as was always our right. The Antaere are masters once again, and it shall remain so until the Final Glory."

EPILOGUE

Three more, along with six pregnancies.
 He couldn't be more pleased.
 Colonel David Cross checked the readings on the meter. *Twenty-two.* That was the highest he'd ever achieved. He wondered if it was due to his excitement with the latest report from Camp Slater?

Although the base was in the process of closing, they were continuing to test the REVs—the Bravos now—for the mutation. Three had tested positive and were currently in route to Earth and his new facility. Add to that the four from Murphy's team, and Cross was building a neat little community of super-Humans.

And the pregnancies. That was the most exciting. From the early successes, there was no doubt the mutation would be passed along. Not one hundred percent, not even fifty. But some would carry the gene through to the next generation. And after that the process would only multiply.

This was just the beginning, at least for this phase. From here on out, there was nothing that could stop him....

THE END

THE REV SAGA CONTINUES...

Zac Murphy's the baddest REV in Corps, but now he's up against an entire galaxy out for his hide...including his own Human race. Not only that, but he's fighting the efforts of the top REV scientist to create a society of super-Humans, all under his control. Zac has faced many a challenge in his life, but this may be more than he can handle.

Now his small team of loyal REVs must stay one step ahead of...well, everyone. Yet when you're borderline super-Human, it's your enemies who have to fear the wrath of the REVs.

REV: RENEGADES

Book 1 of the
REV Warriors Series

REV: Renegades

Now available on Amazon.com

MORE ADAM CAIN ADVENTURES...

And look for the next Adam Cain adventure...

Mission Critical

Part of The Human Chronicles Continuum Series

EMAIL

Please sign up to be included on the master email list to receive updates and announcements regarding the series, including release notices of upcoming books, purchase specials and more, please fill out the **Subscribe** form below:

Subscribe to Email List

CONTACT THE AUTHOR

Email: *bytrharris@hotmail.com*

Website: **bytrharris.com**

NOVELS BY T.R. HARRIS
THE HUMAN CHRONICLES SAGA – CONTINUUM

The Human Chronicles Saga – Continuum
Mission Critical (An Adam Cain Adventure)
The Human Chronicles Saga (original series)
The Fringe Worlds
Alien Assassin
The War of Pawns
The Tactics of Revenge
The Legend of Earth
Cain's Crusaders
The Apex Predator
A Galaxy to Conquer
The Masters of War
Prelude to War
The Unreachable Stars
When Earth Reigned Supreme
A Clash of Aliens
Battlelines
The Copernicus Deception

Novels by T.R. Harris

Scorched Earth
Alien Games
The Cain Legacy
The Andromeda Mission
Last Species Standing
Invasion Force
Force of Gravity

REV Warriors Series
REV
REV: Renegades

Jason King – Agent to the Stars Series
The Enclaves of Sylox
Treasure of the Galactic Lights

The Drone Wars Series
Day of the Drone
In collaboration with George Wier…
The Liberation Series
Captains Malicious

Available exclusively on **Amazon.com**
and **FREE** to members of **Kindle Unlimited**.

Made in the USA
Columbia, SC
26 December 2024